HANG-UPS

ROMANCING THE PHONE #3

MELLANIE SZERETO

Hang-Ups

Published by Amatoria Press
Cover art by Amatoria Press

ISBN: 978-1-942522-95-9

BOOKS BY MELLANIE SZERETO

Cowboys of Science series ~

No More Mr. Gneiss Guy

Creekside series ~

Sexy Claus

Roll With It

Already Gone

Love on the Menu series ~

Love Served Hot

Red Hot Pepper

Hot Tamale Nights (coming soon)

Love on the Menu...Extra Hot standalones ~

Just Desserts

Iced Latté

A Little Appetizer

The Main Dish

Dressing on the Side

Flavor of the Day

Love on the Menu…Steamed trilogy ~

Egging Her On

Sweetening Her Up

Reeling Her In

Love on the Menu: Steamed Boxed Set

Marry Me series ~

Mom I'd Love to Marry

Dad I'd Love to Marry

Nerd Love series ~

Comma Kaze

Nerds & Babies series ~

The Nerd Next Door

The Nerd Upstairs

The Nerd Downstairs

Nerds & Babies Boxed Set

Romancing the Phone series ~

Call Me…Maybe

Smooth Operator

Hang-Ups

Telephone Lines

Dialed Up

Mixed Messages

The Homegrown Café Book Club series ~

Makin' Bacon

The Farmer Takes a Husband

The Butcher and the Baker

When Harry Met Wally

And Baby Makes 2½

The Homegrown Café Book Club Boxed Set

The Jerk Series ~

Jerk in the Box

Jerk of All Trades

Small Town Jerk

Jerk the Ripper

Hit the Jerkpot

Hit the Road, Jerk

Two Forks Hollow Christmas short story series ~

Snowballed

Two Nights Before Christmas

Mistletoe Miscalculation

All Wrapped Up

Standalone Short Stories & Novellas ~

Behind the Mask ~ contemporary romance

Death Benefits ~ paranormal romance

Diner 49er ~ contemporary romcom

Divorce Actually ~ contemporary romcom

Frostbite ~ contemporary holiday romcom

G Marks the Spot ~ contemporary romcom

Karma-lized ~ contemporary romcom

Kiss My Sass ~ contemporary romcom

Mad About You ~ romantic suspense

Not Quite Cupid ~ contemporary romcom

With Bells On ~ contemporary romcom

You Had Me at Goodbye ~ contemporary romcom

The Sextet Anthologies ~

Volume 1: Sharing

Volume 2: Dirty Dancing

Volume 3: Occupational Hazards

Volume 4: Entanglements

Volume 5: Mistletoe & Ménage

The Sextet Presents standalones ~

Playing in the Raine: A Toy Story

Bound by Voodoo: Legends

Bewitching Desires series ~

Two if by Sea

Two Knights of Passion

Two Fated for One

Two Pirates to Treasure

Two Times the Trouble

Two Roped and Ready

Two from the Triangle

Beyond Bewitching

CHAPTER ONE

"RIGHT THERE. YOU NEED TO GO FASTER." A FEMININE groan came from somewhere near the checkout counter. "I can't hold this position much longer."

From his vantage point right inside the front entrance of BOB's Pleasure Palace, Dixon Mayhew could only use his imagination about what was going on between the woman and his most-experienced technician. He wanted sex as much as the next divorced middle-aged man, not that he got any, but doing it during an installation job—even in an adult toy store—violated his work policies. That his employee had a wife and kids while he was screwing around disgusted him even more. He wouldn't have pegged the guy for a cheater. "Rodney."

A clunk preceded another groan, this one obviously belonging to his tech. "Just a sec, boss. Got to make a quick adjustment."

Shaking his head, Dixon waited next to a display filled with every possible size, color, texture, and flavor of lubed and un-lubed condoms on the planet. A tall rack of furry handcuffs stood to the right of it and a shelf of neon orange, pink, and blue vibrators flanked it on the left. He was no prude, but…

A shiny chain caught the light, drawing his eyes to a wide padded band with a buckle at one end and a loop of the same material at the other.

Is that what I think it is?

A headful of silvery-blonde hair popped up beside the shoulder of a black leather bustier-clad mannequin with a spiked collar around her headless neck. Crotchless panties left the very nearly anatomically correct parts at the tops of its cut-off thighs uncovered. When the real woman turned toward him, his dick went from forty-four and mostly limp to eighteen and perpetually horny in less than two seconds.

A strapless Caribbean-aquamarine jumpsuit clung to every one of the bombshell's curves, suggesting beach weather instead of a brewing late-March snowstorm. She slipped her bare feet into feather-adorned heels that added at least three inches to her petite stature. Sexy pink-polished toes peeked out the front of the shoes.

God, the woman had it going on from head to toe.

Chill, dude. Seriously. She's someone's daughter, possibly sister, and maybe granddaughter. Just like Syd.

His daughter would smack him upside the skull for thinking with his other head—and she'd be justified, whether he was suffering from a ridiculously long dry spell or not.

His employee rose behind the counter and tucked a pair of needle-nosed pliers into his back pocket. "The wiring's in for the upgraded surveillance system. It took the two of us almost twenty minutes to thread the damn line past the— *Darn*. Sorry about the cursing, ma'am. Anyway, it's ready to test the video feed."

They were feeding wires, not fucking each other's brains out. Get your brain out of the gutter.

She extended her hand toward Dixon as she crossed to him. "No worries, Rodney. My language is usually much more colorful. You must be Mr. Mayhew. I'm Cerise Wethers, the proprietor of BOB's Pleasure Palace. We spoke on the phone a few weeks ago."

Her professional manner seemed at odds with her husky voice and the sexpot persona she physically conveyed, not to mention the name of her adult toy store. Then again, why couldn't a woman exude confidence, intelligence, beauty, and loads of sex appeal all at the same time?

Closing his much-larger hand around hers, he kept his gaze locked on her face. Hopefully, his coat hid any evidence that he'd been looking elsewhere. "Ms. Wethers, it's good to finally meet you. Call me Dixon."

"Dixon." She nodded once, withdrew her hand, and set off at a brisk walk toward the rear of the shop. "Follow me. My office is in the back room. I really appreciate your willingness to complete the job while the shop is closed."

"I'll finish up here, Rodney. You can head out as soon as you're done loading up. Things are getting nasty out there." He trailed after her, his leisurely pace allowing him to keep up with her and focus on the conversation instead of her swaying hips. "Rod and I are both early risers, so it works well for us. With commercial projects, we prefer to install before or after business hours. When we work on the new system for your house, we'll shift to regular eight-to-five hours."

"Okay." Not slowing, she pushed through the wide employees-only door and veered to the right past three large unopened boxes. Then she flipped on the light switch as she entered a decent-sized space with a functional desk and a lavish seating area. "I take alternating Mondays and Tuesdays off. We can discuss how to handle the interior components after you're finished testing everything here. Would you like a cup of coffee?"

"Yes, thank you. Black's fine." A quartet of screens hung on the wall across from the desk, drawing his attention.

"The Keurig and a selection of coffee and tea are on the sideboard. Mugs are there too. If you change your mind about sweetener or creamer, help yourself. Half-and-half is in the mini fridge." After retrieving a clipboard and a laptop from the table between the couch and chairs, she headed toward the doorway. "I'll be unpacking a shipment if you have any questions."

Her casual do-it-yourself instructions annoyed him a little, but he had to admit he admired her polite refusal to play hostess when she had work to do. He did too, for that matter. "Thanks."

A cloud of estrogen remained in the office long after she left him to check the hookups for the monitors and test the feeds to the cameras at the front and rear doors, at the cash register and strategic spots around the retail area, and in the stockroom and office. It left him antsy and wishing he didn't need to inspect every completed job to satisfy his perfectionist gene. Even his high-maintenance ex-wife hadn't drugged a room the way Cerise Wethers did.

A bark of feminine laughter carried from the stockroom into the office, and its owner held a pizza-sized box on the monitor across from where he sat at the desk. Her lips moved like she was talking to somebody, but the feed didn't reveal anyone else in the wide-angle view. She added the box and several more of the same to the cart beside her. Then she tapped a key on the laptop and wrote what seemed to be a checkmark on the top paper of a clipboard.

Despite his curiosity about the item she'd unpacked, he downed another gulp of his coffee and went back to fiddling with the settings for the camera mounted at the customer entrance. After another failed attempt to bring the picture into focus, he headed back out to the sales floor.

His client looked up at him as he walked past her. "Done?"

He didn't slow, more to avoid an estrogen overdose than her question. "No. One of the cameras isn't working properly."

The click of her heels behind him suggested their conversation wasn't over. "Not the one at the checkout counter, I hope. That thing was a beast to wire."

"The front door." He continued through the stockroom and into the store. A near white-out greeted him on the other side of the glass. "I'm going out to my truck to get another camera. Be right back."

Flurries swirled around him on the short jog to the passenger side, making him wish winter had departed early from northeast Ohio. By the time he grabbed a spare from his emergency supply and ducked inside again, snow had managed to blow into his shirt collar and cling to his beard.

Cerise handed him a towel from under the checkout counter. "Looks wicked out there."

He swiped the cloth over his head and neck. "It is. Visibility is about ten feet and I'd guess there's almost an inch of snow already. Hard to tell with all the wind. It might be a good idea to close up and stay put when I'm done swapping out the units. Even if the road crews start now, they're not going to be able to keep up. Give me about five minutes to install the replacement."

The stubborn set of her jaw suggested she planned to argue the need to shut down her shop for the day, but she gave a firm nod and wiggled her ass through the stockroom door.

God, the woman exuded attitude, not unlike his daughter. Too bad he hadn't learned a damn thing from his weakness for self-confident women by marrying and divorcing one and raising another. Of course, Sydney didn't take pleasure in picking fights with him the way his ex-wife had. He'd done something right during Syd's teen years, despite Teri's never-ending criticism and interference.

The lights flickered twice as he positioned the stepstool beneath the malfunctioning camera. Only the bright snow outside kept him from abandoning the task until a day without a blizzard.

Brisk click-click-clicking approached from behind. "All the lights on the old security panel turned red and there's a lockdown message flashing in the armed and disarmed window. I'm fairly certain that's a bad thing."

"How the hell…" Abandoning the camera problem for the moment, he hurried to the main controls located near the delivery entrance in the back. One look at the control box confirmed that the system had gone haywire, most likely from the fluctuation in power and a bad connection.

"Do you know what's wrong with it?" Cerise's voice caressed his skin as if it were a living, breathing entity, triggering a mix of panic and instant hard-on.

Being trapped with the estrogen queen until the winter weather passed might bring an end to his monk-like existence, but he needed a girlfriend less than he needed a flat tire, a dead furnace, and a notification that his mortgage payment was late.

He punched in the access code and pressed the reboot

button. "The old system had some shorts in the wired elements and those may have experienced a power surge. There's no way to override now, even though we're almost ready to switch over to a wifi-based system with an all-new hardwired backup. We'll try a restart and go from there."

The lights flickered again, plunging them into pitch-black darkness.

Well, that didn't go as planned.

The emergency light came on above the exterior door across the room, but it wasn't near enough to do more than cast deep shadows throughout the stockroom.

Backlight outlining her curves in a perfect silhouette, Cerise pivoted away from him. "I have a flashlight in my office. Be right back."

He nixed the idea to follow her the second it popped into his head, especially since the image that accompanied the thought put his hands on her shapely hips. What was wrong with his brain today? "Be careful. I still have a few tools on your desk."

"Thanks for the warning." She kicked off her heels at the doorway and tiptoed into the dark like a mischievous pixie. After several long moments and the sound of a drawer opening and closing, a beam of light lit up a wide swath across the floor. Her ghostlike reappearance took his breath away. "Do you know anyone who installs generators? The kind that kicks on automatically when the power goes out? A standby generator, I think it's called. That's the next upgrade I'm making to the building, even if it costs a bundle. I need more than emergency lighting and a temporary backup for the security system."

"I'll check with a few contractors I trust and let you know by the end of the week." Glad for the distraction, he fished his cell from his pants pocket to add the task to his to-do list." You have access to a gas line, right?"

"Yes." With the light reflecting off the light-colored flooring, her blonde hair formed a halo around her head, the antithesis of the woman she imparted to the public eye. She looked nothing like the suspiciously too-convenient widow some people in town implied or outright accused her of being whenever she became the topic of gossip, especially since both men had been wealthy. As straightforward as she was, using poison to induce heart attacks didn't seem like her style at all. Hell, even a sex-induced aneurysm was far more believable than death by nightshade. "The temperature's going to drop pretty quickly if the power doesn't come back on soon, which isn't likely with this storm. Let's close the window and door shades to block out some of the cold. Then we can go in the office and shut the door since it's the smallest interior room. It should hold the heat longest. Plus, I have drinks, food, and comfortable furniture in there."

He gave a curt nod, glad her practicality tempered his unexpected reaction to her. "Good plan."

Her brisk pace to the front of the store challenged him to keep up, despite her short but shapely legs. She lowered the blinds closest to the checkout counter, blocking out the snowy scene before he reached the other window facing the parking lot. "Do you need to call anybody to let them know you're safe? There probably isn't much cell signal in this weather, but I have a landline for the shop."

Focusing on the job at hand instead of the potential chance to have a date, he shook his head. "Normally, I'd say yes, but my son's on a senior class trip this week. My daughter's in college and won't be home for spring break until Friday."

"No wife? Or significant other?"

Although the question sounded innocent enough, he couldn't help but wonder if she was fishing for information. "Nope. Divorced. No girlfriend."

The blinds on the entrance snapped at the bottom of the glass as Cerise seemed to look him up and down. After locking both deadbolts on the door, she grabbed a package of batteries and a box from one of the displays on her way back through the shop. "Hurry up. And before you ask, I got the condoms just in case. Hard to say how long the power will be out. I get bored easily."

He followed the wedge of light into the stockroom and toward her office, unsure whether he should be thrilled by the possibility of real sex for the first time in years or scared because of her casual mention of it. No way in hell would he be able to resist her invitation. The heavy *thunk* of the door closing behind him rang through the space like a hammer hitting the final nail in a coffin.

I'm fucked.

Well, not yet, but probably at some point.

She placed the batteries and the box of condoms on the coffee table—in plain sight until such time as she decided to turn off the flashlight—and gestured for him to sit on the couch. An unexpected smile curved her pink lips upward. "You should see your expression. Don't worry. I'm not going to jump your boner without your permission. Yes, I notice those things about men, especially since they can't exactly hide it. We may as well get comfortable."

Heat crawled across his face, assuring him he'd blushed. "I didn't mean to think about you in that way."

Her smile morphed into a wicked grin. "Why not? I'm thinking about you in *that way*. I'm single. You're single. We can have sex with each other if we want to, and I would never feel guilty for bringing myself or someone else pleasure. Have a seat. I promise not to bite. Nibbling is another story."

He dropped into the chair, not trusting her to keep her hands, mouth, and other body parts to herself any more than he could. "I don't sleep with every woman I meet."

"I don't sleep with every man I meet. Maybe I just want to make lubricated balloon animals." She winked at him a moment before she perched on the table facing him, her legs between his knees, and clicked off the flashlight.

CHAPTER TWO

CERISE SET ASIDE THE FLASHLIGHT AND RESTED HER HANDS on Dixon's thighs. The immediate tightening of his muscles and a croaked groan confirmed she hadn't misread the attraction in his expressive brown eyes.

The man was unimaginatively predictable—intimidated by her frankness—but cute. She liked his slightly prudish sense of propriety and the fact that he hadn't leered at her, tried to cop a feel, or used a pickup line like the vast majority of men she met. They rarely expected her to be a blonde with a brain and a backbone. A bimbo with no standards was more like it.

Dixon Mayhew had superb thighs, in addition to a pleasant personality. Black-framed glasses gave him a studious look that made her want to know if they hid a passionate man behind the handsome and slightly geeky exterior.

Curiosity tempted her jump him right then and there so she could find out if his chinstrap beard and moustache scraped, tickled, or caressed sensitive places on her body.

His breathing came in rough inhales and exhales,

suggesting he fully expected her to pounce on him at any second.

"How long were you married?" She followed his tense muscles a few inches higher before moving her hands to the chair, where he clenched the armrests. She stifled a laugh at the way he jumped from the brief brush of her fingertips on his wrists.

"Wha-at?" His cracking voice triggered a tiny surge of sympathy for him.

"How long were you married?" She loosened each clamped finger, rubbing the callouses on each one and imagining how amazing they would feel on her body. They spoke of a man who spent more time running his business on the job than from behind a desk.

His rough swallow broke the silence. "Fourteen years. Too long. You?"

He'd clearly heard the small-town gossip about at least one of her short-lived nuptials. Whether he believed the stories about how she'd become widowed twice in four years remained to be seen.

She closed her eyes and focused the feel of his skin against hers, the rhythm of his steadier breathing, and his subtle masculine scent—all but one of the things she missed about having a man in her life. If she lucked out, she might share a few orgasms with the owner of Tech Minds, Incorporated. "Almost a year and a half the first time. Ten months the second time. Not quite three years between marriages. You know I'm a widow, don't you? Twice."

"Is that supposed to scare me off? Or is it a warning? You don't really strike me as a praying-mantis type of woman."

"Just stating the facts. And for the record, I would never rip off a man's head after sex unless he made it all about him."

After a low chuckle, he slipped his fingers through hers and gave a gentle squeeze. "I may not mean to listen, but people in Bell like to gossip while I'm working—to me and on the phone and in person to their friends. I think they're looking for a reason to dislike the woman who's self-confident enough to run a store they're all curious about."

"And jealous because my dead husbands left me a shit-load of money for not cheating on them." A hint of bitterness seeped into her statement, something that rarely happened, even when she got together with her closest friends for happy hour and to shoot the shit. "Tell me about your kids. Unless you'd rather skip to the fun stuff. FYI, the couch folds out into a pretty comfortable bed. I'm not sure how sturdy it is for sex since I've only ever slept in it alone."

His breathing stuttered again and his fingers flexed. "I—"

The landline phone on her desk drowned out whatever he might have said next.

She withdrew her right hand to grab the flashlight and switch it on. Avoiding his gaze, she stood. "I should get that while you think about your options."

His release of her other hand brought a brief sensation of loss, catching her off guard. She frowned as she crossed to the phone. She didn't miss men or dating at all. The toys from her store gave her a new partner whenever the mood hit and created none of the drama that had plagued her life since Tony Hopkins, deceased husband number one, had kicked the bucket on his forty-fourth birthday.

Pushing the memory from her thoughts, she picked up the receiver. "BOB's Pleasure Palace. How may we improve your sex life?"

A muffled choke came from Dixon's direction, joining Rose Holloway's familiar snicker in her ear. "Mine is pretty damn spectacular. Hey, Cerise. Barton saw your car at the shop on his way home from the gas station about an hour ago. Just wondering if you tried to drive home and checking to make sure you're okay."

"Hi, Rose. The power's out, but I'll be fine. My hot flashes will keep me warm."

Her friend snorted. "Barton also said Dixon Mayhew's TMI truck was in the parking lot. I'm guessing you'll be keeping *each other* warm—and occupied—if he's still there. Is he?"

The direct question didn't surprise Cerise. Her friends didn't beat around the bush when they wanted answers. "Yes, but I don't know what I'm doing about it yet."

"Take advantage of the situation. He's smart, nice, and good-looking. Single. Most women would jump at the chance to get snowed in with a guy like him. And you have an endless supply of condoms and toys. I want to hear all about your adventures at our next get-together."

"Of course you do. I'll let you know if I need you to send out Barton and a rescue team." Cerise crossed her fingers Rose got the hint to drop the subject, but she wasn't about to hold her breath.

"Your house. Sunday night. I'm bringing a pot of soup. Scarlet's picking up some bread from the bakery, Poppy's making brownies, Sienna wants to try a drunken-fruit recipe one of her clients gave her, and I'm still waiting to hear back from Carnie about what booze she's bringing. You're supplying the venue and the scandalous stories. They better be good."

Barely resisting a glance at Dixon, Cerise lifted her chin and squared her shoulders. "Have I ever let you down? Go snuggle with your husband and enjoy a day off."

"Go hump the hunk and have some cheery Os. Full report on Sunday."

The dial tone hummed in Cerise's ear for several seconds before she returned the receiver to its base. Scandalous had been her middle name through high school, undergrad, and grad school. Even her thirties and early forties fit the description.

The last five years?

Not so much.

Self-induced orgasms had become her go-to method after Bradley Yeats had gone to sleep with a smile on his face and never awakened. Having two husbands croak right after sex had put quite the damper on her dating life, not that she planned to do more than hook up with her high-tech security guy.

Since when do I overthink getting naked with a man I'm attracted to?

"Everything okay?" Dixon's question pulled her out of her thoughts with its edge of concern.

She nodded and moved to the sideboard to light a tropical-scented candle. "Rose Holloway was checking on me. She was still Rose Chambers when you upgraded the system at Bell Lumber last fall. She and Barton got married right before Christmas."

"I heard. Scarlet Brinks. Rose. The gossips are taking bets on which one of your friends is next." His fingers flexed and then relaxed as she sat on the couch with the table between them. "Their money's on Poppy Gardner."

"Really? They're not speculating about who I'm trapping in my web next? Hm. I guess I need to up my game, although the rumor mill should have plenty of fodder when word gets around that you and I were snowed in together. May as well live up to their expectations, don't you agree?"

His lips curved into a wide grin. "They're going to have to be disappointed since I have no plans to get married again.

Not that I believe you had anything to do with your late husbands' deaths."

"But I did." She waited for the inevitable frown and narrow-eyed stare, but he chuckled and sat back in the chair instead, suddenly looking far more at ease than he had five minutes ago.

"Uh-uh. I recognize that attempt at the shock factor. My daughter perfected it when she was seven." The challenge in his gaze set off a pair of successive tremors in her lower belly.

Foreplay?

Stretching out on the sofa, she exhaled and willed away the pressure in her lower spine. Her fifty-first birthday last month shouldn't have gifted her muscle spasms in her back when she sat at her desk for more than two hours at a time like she had earlier. "Shock factor, huh? They both died from heart-related causes within an hour of having sex with me. And, no, they weren't twice my age. I was the same age as my first husband and older by two years the second time around. They were both forty-four."

"You mean…you were in bed with them when it happened? You discovered…" His voice dropped closer to a whisper with every word. "Damn. That must've been pretty traumatic for you. And to have it happen twice. I'm sorry about the shock factor remark."

She shrugged and focused on the dancing shadows from the candle. "No worries. I don't hold grudges."

"You just get even?"

"Not worth the effort. Besides, I trust karma to keep score." She flexed her hips, triggering an audible pop near her tailbone. Then her knees cracked as she pulled them to her chest and exhaled again. "Mmm. Much better."

The chair across from her creaked. "Are you okay? My

chiropractor recommended some exercises for relieving lower-back pain when I sit for too long."

"Nothing some stretching and physical activity won't fix. Can't do anything about hypermobile hips except take advantage of my flexibility." A glance in his direction confirmed her suspicions. His cheeks had flushed a healthy shade of pink and his hands clenched the armrests again. "You know, there's nothing wrong with thinking and talking about sex. Or engaging in it. How long?"

"How—" He cleared his throat of the pubescent teenage-boy squeak. "How long what?"

She pressed her lips together to suppress a giggle and swung her legs around to sit up. "Well, let's see. How long since you've had sex? How long since you've kissed a woman? How long is your…drive home?"

Shoving his fingers through his hair, he stood. After three steps toward the darkest part of the room, he pivoted to face her and took a noisy breath. "Eight."

Her snicker became a hoot of laughter when his lips twitched and formed a grin. "Now you're getting it! I can't remember the last time a man entertained me with something that wasn't sex-related. Maybe I won't have to open that box of condoms to keep from being bored."

"For the record, I didn't say I was opposed to that." He leaned his hip against the corner her desk, his posture almost cocky. "Eight years since sex. Roughly eight months since a peck on the cheek and eight years since I swapped spit. Eight minutes with normal traffic and good weather. Before you ask, I'd say eight inches, but I've never measured it."

Warmth not caused by a hot flash spread through her chest and belly for the first time in forever. She'd almost forgotten how true attraction felt. "I like your sense of humor, Dixon. You're not as uptight as you pretend to be."

He shrugged. "I've been focusing on work and parenting for most of the last decade. I'm out of practice flirting and interacting with women in a social setting. Not that I was ever a ladies' man. Too geeky for the popular girls. Glasses and braces didn't help, either."

"Looks are mostly genetics, something we can't control. Character is far more important." Suddenly restless, she stood and headed for the sideboard. "Brains are sexy—when moderated by humility. Want something to drink? Water? Juice? Sorry, no way to make more coffee and I don't keep alcohol in the shop."

"Nothing for me. Thanks." His gaze seemed to bore a hole in her back as she filled a glass at the dispenser. "Men—and women, for that matter—clearly judge you based on your appearance, but I'm curious about your intellectual side. You're smart. I think there's more to you than meets the eye. Tell me about Cerise Wethers."

She took a long swallow of water while she debated sharing what few people in Bell knew about her. Would his opinion about her widow-ness change?

Returning to the couch gave her several seconds to consider her response. She blew out a quiet exhale as she placed her glass on the coffee table beside the batteries and condoms. "I was a pharmacist before I met Bradley and Tony. Top of my class. Worked for a major drug company for twenty years and decided to go back to school for a business degree. It caused quite a stir when the coroner found out I knew exactly how to make a poisoning look like a heart attack. What started out as a second case of heart failure when Bradley died became an investigation that included toxicology reports and lots of questions. Then came the suspicions about Tony's death. A chat with their cardiologists confirmed what the medical examiner found and convinced the police to close both cases. I was cleared, but not everybody believes they died from natural causes."

Dixon walked back to the chair, his expression unreadable in the dim light, even after he sat across from her again. "I thought I had a good reason for never wanting to get remarried. You don't, do you? Want to get remarried again, that is."

"Not a chance." A shudder rippled along her spine at the mere thought of walking down the aisle a third time. "And I'm most certainly not having sex with a forty-four-year-old man ever again."

His eyebrows dipped toward his nose and his mouth formed a frown. "We're not going to need that box of condoms then."

A very unladylike snort summed up her feelings about that revelation. "You're forty-four, huh? Of course you are. This just keeps getting better and better."

He laughed, but the sound held more pain than amusement. "If it's any consolation, my birthday is tomorrow."

"So I should hope for a snowstorm and power outage that lasts at least another fifteen hours? That's a lot of foreplay."

"Yeah. I'm pretty sure my tongue would cramp and fall off, but it would be worth it to give you a happy ending." A dimple, barely discernible in the candlelight, formed in his left cheek above his sexy scruff as his lips curved upward. "It's been probably fifteen years since the last time I ate a woman for dessert."

Her nipples puckered against the lace of her strapless bra, and a rush of heat and dampness flooded the juncture of her thighs. Not even the latest and greatest vibrator in her suppliers' catalogues inspired that kind of reaction. "You know what they say. Practice makes perfect."

CHAPTER THREE

DIXON WILLED HIS MUSCLES INTO SUBMISSION, HOPING HIS zipper didn't split wide open. He barely stopped himself from jumping over the table to bury his face between Cerise's legs. Had he ever in his life wanted anyone as much as he wanted her?

Living like a monk had sucked, but he'd never been tempted to fuck a woman right after meeting her. He also didn't talk dirty to women. At least he hadn't until Cerise Wethers.

His dick throbbed, threatening his self-control more with every passing second.

Her implied invitation still hung in the air and shone in her parted lips and smoldering eyes. "Help me fold out the sofa. This floor is hell on the knees."

Not sure he could speak if his life depended, he nodded and rose. The motion necessary for moving the coffee table confirmed his hard-on had reached full mast and then some. Bending wasn't a viable option unless he released the beast.

Not my best idea.

He let out a slow breath to ease the tension in his jaw as she pulled the table out of the way and turned toward him.

"You look like you're in pain." Her gaze dropped from his to somewhere below his chest. "Maybe you should take off your pants while I make the bed. I think somebody wants to come out and play."

When she licked her lips, his dick twitched in another attempt to break free, cutting off the circulation to his brain.

"Or I can do it for you." She slipped her hand between the cushions at the back of couch and tugged on a loop of fabric, transforming the seating area into a bedroom. "We definitely need some mutual oral stimulation for round one. I have a feeling it'll be a quick trip for both of us."

Round one.

Mutual oral stimulation.

His racing pulse echoed in his ears. "I'll do it. The minute you touch me, I'm a goner."

A grin spread across her face as she lifted the seat of his chair, pulled two pillows from a hidden compartment, and tossed them onto the already-made bed. "This is going to be a very productive power outage."

Ignoring the voice in the head with his brain that told him to suck in the little bit of dad gut he'd gained over the last several years, he unbuttoned his company shirt and yanked it over his head. Nerdy middle-aged men rarely looked like bodybuilders. He was no exception. His hand stalled with his pants unfastened and partway unzipped.

The brainy bombshell shimmied out of her jumpsuit, leaving her in a lacy strapless bra and underwear nearly the same color as her skin. He itched to explore every inch of her, an experience completely new to him. How had he gone a day shy of forty-five years without feeling that kind of attraction—desire so strong his whole body ached from the need to physically connect with her?

She stretched out on the covers on her stomach, propping herself up on her elbows and giving him a perfect view of her delectable cleavage. "Unless you changed your mind, you need to hurry up."

Instead of answering, he kicked off his shoes and stripped out of the rest of his clothes. His rock-hard erection lurched upward in celebration of its newfound freedom. Cool air slowed the heat thrumming through his veins, but the fire remained.

Her silvery hair tumbled past her bare shoulder, hiding half of one sparkling eye from him. Then she rolled over and flicked open the clasp between her breasts. The lace clung to the full mounds as she hooked her thumbs in the matching barely there panties. "It's a damn shame you've been keeping that equipment all to yourself."

His breath caught in his lungs as she pushed the delicate scrap of fabric and elastic past the curves of her hips. A triangle of light-colored curls assured him she was a natural blonde, not that her hair color was a deal-breaker. Everything about her was real, however, right down to her straightforward personality.

And I don't have to hold myself back with her.

Letting his dick rule his actions, he climbed onto the bed and released her imprisoned flesh so she was every bit as naked as he was. Her nipples puckered into tight buds, and her eyelids fluttered closed for a several seconds. His mouth watered, compelling him to lick a taut pink tip while he palmed her other breast.

Her breathy moan sounded loud in the private space they shared. "Give me that cock."

He pushed aside the inclination to overthink, swung his

leg over her head, and positioned his face inches above her spread-eagle thighs. Balancing on his right forearm, he slicked his middle finger through her folds. Her sweet scent swirled around him, intoxicating him more than the estrogen cloud that followed her everywhere. “I love eating pussy.”

She sucked his balls between her lips, the gentle suction moving them in a sea of wet heat and threatening to make him shoot his load. “Mmm.”

“Fuck.” Determined to take her with him, he swiped his tongue along the earlier path he’d taken and glided his finger inside her, following spasming muscles and the curve of her slippery channel to what he hoped was her G-spot.

Her strangled groan accompanied the sudden pressure of lips and a tongue around his length. Then her teeth scraped along the sensitive spot near the head of his erection, ending the tentative control he hadn’t really had.

An eruption of epic proportions rushing in, he fluttered his tongue over her swollen clit and finger-fucked her like the world was ending. A growl rumbled up his throat and blended with a muffled cry as they both tensed. Weightlessness and euphoria carried him away with her for countless minutes before he finally floated back to the reality.

He dropped to the mattress beside her, his heart pounding and his breathing ragged. Tremors registered where his hand rested on her calf, a sure sign he’d given her a fair share of pleasure too.

“Damn.” She shuddered, shaking the entire bed. “Sex may kill *me* this time.”

That she could joke about the possibility shattered any exhilaration still lingering in his body and mind. No wonder she’d avoided relationships. Waking up to a dead spouse once had to have been horrific, but twice had clearly played a number on her ability to even interact with men.

Abrupt movement warned him the moment had quickly dissipated for her too. Her shadow moved along the wall opposite the burning candle. "Those words were funnier in my head."

Despite the bucket of cold water she'd dumped on the afterglow, he crawled to the pillows and folded back the blankets. "Come back to bed. If you want to talk, we'll talk. If not, we can take a nap or discuss round two."

Her curvy silhouette stopped near the door to the stockroom. "Round two. How do you feel about toys? I have a closet full of samples. Vibrators, nipple clamps, cock rings, restraints. We can participate in a lot of sexually satisfying activities that don't include intercourse. Always consensual, of course."

His cock twitched to life again, obviously interested in the prospect of trying out her supply of props. He lifted the covers as an invitation. "I don't have the benefit of hot flashes to keep me warm. How about sharing some of that body heat? I promise to make it worth your while, and I'll answer your question."

"I'm pretty sure I can guess." The shadow distorted as she moved closer. With a single quick puff, she extinguished the candle, plunging the room into total darkness. A few seconds later, she slipped in beside him and tickled his neck with her breath. "Do you like toys, Dixon?"

The way his dick stood at attention, he was certain it was interested in whatever she suggested. Her sultry voice didn't hurt, either.

Needing the silky feel of her skin against his, he guided her head to his chest and wrapped his arm around her shoulders. "I've led an unremarkable sex life, so I can't say for sure, but I'm willing to be adventurous with you. My dick has no objections."

Her palm caressed a path past his ribs and over his stomach to the base of his growing erection. She traced the vein up his shaft, making his main brain short-circuit. "Nice recovery time. Are you sure you're ready to go again?"

"I think my hard-on speaks for itself." He moved his hand from her waist to her ass and slid his leg between hers. Inching higher, he didn't stop until she ground herself into his thigh. "Are you?"

She closed her fist around him and pumped down and back up, bringing him fully erect. Then her mouth covered his nipple and she sucked. "Mm-hm."

A riot of sensations ricocheted straight to his balls, through his cock, and to every nerve ending in his body. He groaned and rocked his hips upward, wanting more of her touch. "God, those hands and that mouth. The toys can wait."

She chuckled while her tongue circled his tight bud. "Uh-uh. Reach under the pillow. One of my favorites is under there. Slide it on your finger and push the power button when you're ready. It's fully charged."

As much as he enjoyed holding on to her gorgeous butt, the opportunity to get her off with one of her vibrators was too good to pass up. Following her instructions, he quickly had the device positioned at the first knuckle of his thumb but not yet powered on.

After a flick of her tongue over his surprisingly sensitive nipple, she raised her head. "Find my clit and hold the bumpy side there. Stay in the same spot once I tell you where to hold it. I prefer steady pressure. And if you make me come first, I'll use it on you."

What felt like an electrical shock swept through him, radiating outward from his testicles to his fingers, toes, and the hair on his head. Her sexual experience definitely outweighed his, not that he minded. If she wanted to lead their extracurricular activities, he wouldn't argue.

"I won't be able to concentrate on figuring out how this thing works with you jacking me off at the same time." He carefully extracted his cock from her grip and laid her on her back as he got to his knees. Not even a faint outline of her naked form gave him a clue where to start. "This would be easier if I could see what I'm doing."

"Do you want easy, or do you want to learn what makes your partner feel amazing?" She feathered the arch of her foot along his calf, inciting a surge of goose bumps up to his groin. "The senses are amplified in the dark. I can't see where you are, but I can feel your presence and I can tell you're close to me. Don't get me wrong. I love sex with the lights on. There's just something about using touch, sound, smell, and taste to enhance the experience and memorize your lover's body."

She made a damn good point.

"Okay, teacher, teach me."

Instead of laughing at his ineptitude, she withdrew her foot. "Create an image of me in your mind. Where am I on the bed? In what position? Can you hear me breathing or moving against the sheets? Do you smell my shampoo? My bodywash? Can you tell if I'm aroused by my scent? Use all of those elements and your own intuition to explore and discover. Let my pheromones guide you. You don't need to see me."

He closed his eyes and tried to picture her lying tangled in the sheets and blankets he'd held back to welcome her into the bed. Were her arms stretched out over head? Or was she cupping her breasts and teasing her nipples? Or maybe she was playing with her clit.

A faint shoosh hinted that she'd moved against the

bedding, and the hairs on his leg told him she lay a mere fraction of an inch from his skin.

I bet my dick can find her pussy in the dark.

The smoky remnants of the burning candle lingered in the air, but the salty-sweet essence of her desire drew his attention lower, somewhere near his knee if he wasn't mistaken.

Without opening his eyes, he reached for her, connecting with silky-smooth skin and a subtle dip. Her pelvic bone greeted him as he followed the narrow ledge higher. At least that's what his mind saw. To confirm the thought, he continued upward, finding the curved outline of her ribs.

Her soft sigh added to the eroticism that made him willing to end his eight-year commitment to celibacy. "Yes. Nice and slow. Sex isn't always about Part P in Part V. Delayed gratification can lead to sustained and more intense pleasure when the moment finally…comes."

He relied on tactile imagery to guide him to the swell of her breast. Its warmth permeated his fingertips and palm, despite the slightly cooler air than an hour ago. Using his forefinger, he pushed the indentation of the vibrator to turn it on. A few inches more, and he found her tightly puckered nipple with his humming thumb. "Delayed gratification. Blow jobs, hand jobs, and battery-powered toys are all well and good, but I'm in dire need of sex with you in the traditional sense. How long until midnight?"

Cerise and the bed quivered, her barely audible gasp alerting him that something he'd said or done had triggered a reaction in her. "Fifteen? Maybe sixteen hours?"

A groan crawled up his throat. "Can we skip ahead to making each other come again? I'm about ready to explode from thinking about fucking you until neither of us can move."

She whimpered, summing up his exact mood. Then her

hand closed over his and moved it down her body. "Lesson one is over. We'll pick up where we left off when we start lesson two after a short recess. Right there. Oh, good thinking. Are you sure you've never used this kind of vibe before?"

He added a second finger to her slick channel, careful not to stray from the spot she'd indicated, and grunted as he touched his lips to where his gut imagined her nipple rested atop a perfect handful of flesh.

Bingo.

Hoping the triple action worked its magic in a hurry, he thrust and buzzed and alternately sucked and licked in a steady rhythm, relishing her erratic breathing and uninhibited moans.

"I wish you could touch me everywhere. Press a little harder. Yes, like that." Her muscles trembled around him and she arched upward. "So damn close. Don't stop. Yes, yes, *yes*!"

Her whole body jerked and tensed as she cried out, but he didn't stop—wouldn't until she told him to. The sounds she made went on and on, threatening to take him over the edge with her.

She finally went limp, nudging the hand with the vibrator away. "Holy hell. I don't think. I've ever. Come. That hard. Before. Give me. A minute."

Resting his arm across her quaking belly while knowing where their bodies touched without the benefit of light, he grinned. "You're so fucking sexy. Take two. Or three. I'm not going anywhere."

CHAPTER FOUR

HER PULSE NO LONGER ECHOED IN HER EARS AND EUPHORIA tried to drag toward sleep, but Cerise had no intention of letting Dixon's balls turn blue. He'd earned a first-rate battery-assisted ejaculation that equaled the orgasm he'd given her, and she couldn't wait to blow his mind.

She ran her palm along his muscular forearm to his wrist, pausing for a moment before continuing to his thumb to slip the lavender mini vibe free. "You've been very patient. Ready for your turn?"

His shaky exhale caressed her shoulder. "I can't say I won't embarrass myself, but I'm ready."

"There's no reason to be embarrassed. It doesn't matter how fast or slow you get off. Pleasure is the goal." She slipped the Purple Pulser onto her middle finger and levered up to her hands and knees beside him, still a bit shaky from having him rock her world. Starting on the lowest setting, she found and cradled his balls, lightly squeezing as vibrations hummed through his sac. "Tell me if you like what I'm doing. If it's too much or not enough. Whether you want me to move or hold it in one place. Lower or higher speed. Talk to me, Dixon."

He blew out a brisk huff. "Nice. I like it. Maybe a little higher speed. Yeah, right there. God, I wish you had more hands."

She stifled a smirk in case his senses had become more attuned to her body and emotions in the dark. *No need to make him overthink.* "Into threesomes, are you?"

The choking sound he made and the instant change in his cock hinted at his thoughts about that scenario. "No."

"You know, it's okay to have fantasies." She moved the vibe along the seam between his balls to the vein running up his rock-hard length. "Do you have fantasies? Being with two women? A woman and a man? A man? It's normal, especially when your sex life has consisted of solo orgasms for years."

He groaned. "Okay, okay. I've imagined being with two women, but I'd never actually do it. Would you?"

Following the hard ridge, she stopped right below the head and bumped up the speed another notch. "Two women? No, only one and only once. It was during my experimental undergrad years. Not really my thing, although she was very good at oral. Definitely in the top twenty of orgasms."

"Fuck, that's hot." His dick twitched and he blew out another noisy breath. "What about two guys? A guy and a girl?"

"So you *do* have fantasies." She smoothed a hand along his firm abdominal muscles in a search for more erogenous body parts to play with. A smattering of chest hair ignited tingles in her fingertips as she explored the territory she'd licked and sucked during round one. The first brush over his taut nipple earned her a rumbly groan. "Both. I've found that I prefer to have at least half of the attention during sex. Two men works for me if they're not into each other, but I've stuck to one man at a time since I turned thirty. Would you have liked watching me have sex with a woman or as part of a threesome? Or maybe you would've liked being part of it. Tell me about your deepest desires, even if you would never act on them."

His heart beat strong and steady beneath her palm, despite his rough breathing. "Not sure how I feel about sharing, but I'm damn sure I couldn't watch without touching you. Right now, all I can think about is how much I want to be inside you. Fucking you hard and fast, slow and deep, for hours and days, making us both come over and over and over."

She flicked her tongue across his tight bud as she bumped up the speed again. "Would you want to watch me masturbate? I do that almost every day. Gotta try out all these toys."

He grunted, his control obviously slipping. "Yes. In person. Over FaceTime. And I'd jack off while I was watching you."

His gravelly voice reignited her temporarily sated libido in an instant, but she wasn't about to short-change him on a solo ride to Orgasmville. "But would you just watch? Or would you want to join me? Help me take everything for a test drive? Then I wouldn't have to imagine having a partner while I fucked my pussy with a—"

A choked roar drowned out the rest of her words and a spurt of warm fluid landed on her lips. Instead of immediately licking off the treat, she sucked on his stiff nipple to prolong his release. More droplets splatted on her upper arm near her elbow. "Mmm."

Harsh panting ruffled her hair for at least a full minute, and his grip on her ass slowly loosened. "Jesus. Sex was never this good before."

Satisfaction washed over her in gentle waves. "Then we'll

have to be sure you get plenty more to make up for lost opportunities."

He stilled. "How much more? Like even after we're not trapped by a freak snowstorm and a power outage?"

Although he sounded curious rather than demanding, a flash of unease raced up her spine. She worked to keep her tone casual but firm. "I'm not interested in a relationship, Dixon. No dating, no boyfriend, and definitely no romantic involvement."

"Not an issue. My attitude toward women is probably just as fucked up as your attitude toward men. I love my kids, but my marriage was a huge mistake. I don't think the two of us using each other for mutual orgasms would be. We both want the same thing."

Relief tried to creep in, but she needed to be sure. "A friends-with-benefits arrangement, you mean? A booty call where nobody gets hurt."

"Yes, exactly." His hand closed around hers, shutting off and removing the mini vibe from her finger. "I'm serious. I'd like to have a safe and reliable partner for sex without the complications of the inevitable breakup. A partner I like as a friend. Someone who agrees to keep things casual and understands that the happy ending happens in bed, not with a wedding."

She exhaled and let the tension dissipate from her shoulders. "Exclusive—because having multiple partners increases the risk of STDs exponentially—but with no expectations except phenomenal sex. I can do that."

"I agree about being exclusive, not that I have the time or ambition to juggle a bunch of women. Or even two. Besides, I doubt I'd ever meet anyone else who could hold a candle to your skills and knowledge."

Chemistry has more to do with it than book smarts. Of

course, she couldn't actually tell him that without sounding like she thought they had some sort of connection.

He dragged the covers over top of them and guided her head back to the firm pillow of his right pec. "I don't know about you, but I need to recharge."

Letting his cool skin soothe the heat rapidly fanning out over her upper back and chest, she closed her eyes. "Mm-hmm."

His arm tensed where it was draped around her waist. "Are you okay? You're really hot all of a sudden. Your skin. I'm pretty sure you're always hot, but… God, what a jackass line. Forget I said that."

A chuckle snuck out and she couldn't help but smile against him. "I'll take that as the compliment it was meant to be. It's just a hot flash."

"Need some water or something?"

The concern in his voice confirmed what she already suspected. Dixon Mayhew was a nice guy, a man worthy of her attention—in a good way.

She relaxed into him, enjoying the coarse hair beneath her cheek. "No, thanks. It should pass in a couple minutes. In the meantime, take advantage of the heat."

He rolled her on top of him, adjusting the blankets once they lay skin to skin and he'd tangled their legs together. One of his hands rested a few inches above her ass and the other rubbed slow circles along her spine. "Better. The temperature feels like it's dropped at least five degrees since the power went out."

"Not surprised with the way the wind was blowing." A yawn escaped, reminding she'd gotten out of bed at four thirty instead the usual six in the morning.

He followed suit, proving the action was catching. "Ready for a catnap?"

His steady heartbeat in her ear, the aftereffects of shared orgasms, and the waning of the hot flash lulled her toward sleep, but she managed a grin. "Yes, my pussy needs a short rest."

Rumbling laughter echoed through her pitch-black office and shook her like a massive earthquake. The man wearing her as a blanket wasn't the prude she'd first pegged him to be—not even close. He wasn't intimidated by her bluntness or her sex drive, and he evidently appreciated her uninhibited sense of humor.

His outburst finally quieted to soft chuckles. "I don't think boredom is going to be an issue while we're stuck here."

"Definitely not." She wiggled a little to the left to keep her breast from being smooshed, and his semi-stiff cock made contact with her inner thigh. The man certainly had the kind of stamina she could appreciate. "Close your eyes and go to sleep, Dixon."

He flattened his palm near the middle of her back and yawned again. "Yes, ma'am."

"Smartass."

"Yep." Another yawn made his chest rise and fall, but he held her in place when she might have wobbled. Then his breathing evened out into slow inhales and exhales.

She closed her own eyes and focused on his masculine scent, the rhythm of his heart in her ear, and the feel of his body everywhere they made contact. His hold eased as the seconds and minutes ticked by, though he didn't let go. She'd missed post-coital touching in the dark, the relaxation that accompanied coming down from the high of physical release.

Her muscles went slack as time passed, but sleep eluded her. She didn't need a shrink to know why. One time waking up next to a dead lover had been disturbing. Twice in a lifetime more than exceeded overkill. As much as she wanted the-real-deal sex, ghosts of husbands past—and passed—haunted her thoughts and warned her not to take her friends-with-benefits arrangement too far.

Dixon rolled to his right, taking her with him. His calloused fingertips skimmed over hip and down to her knee. A contented sigh ruffled her hair and he snuggled closer, guiding her leg to his waist—which put his hairy thigh in direct contact with her bare crotch. His wake-up woody twitched against her belly. After a husky hum and another slow exhale, he stilled.

A flash of desire awoke the body parts that might argue about what constituted "too far."

Is it intercourse? Or is it a sleepover after intercourse?

Waking in the arms of a man had led to morning part-P-in-part-V sex on numerous occasions up until the untimely demise of Bradley, but those days were over. The third-times-the-charm adage could mean ending up on the murder end of a suspicious-death charge as easily as breaking the curse the universe had placed on her.

The Blonde Widow. It has a catchy ring to it if you're into that kind of thing. At least they can't call me the love-'em-and-cleave-'em type.

However, being the featured killer on a true-crime podcast wasn't on her bucket list.

Did she regret seducing Dixon?

No. Regretting multiple orgasms is like wishing you hadn't won the lottery.

Yes, consequences and complications sometimes accompanied both, but everybody needed a little immediate gratification now and then.

I never overthink my decisions. What the hell is menopause doing to me?

She eased a few inches away and lost the distance when he tugged her flush with his torso and erection again.

He closed his hand over her ass, trapping her right where her traitorous body wanted to be. “Where’re you going?”

His sleep-roughened words sauntered along her spine, sending her hormones into a frenzy. She swallowed to wet her suddenly parched throat, the only part of her that had dried up from the sound of his rumbly voice. “To see what time it is, go to the bathroom, and to get a drink.”

“Careful you don’t stub those pretty little toes.” He slowly loosened his hold. “And hurry back. We need to conserve body heat.”

A whimper almost escaped as she scooted toward the edge of the bed. He was too damn sexy and thoughtful—the perfect man for sharing orgasms with and nothing more.

Chilly air met her skin, but it barely cooled the fire he’d stoked and continued to fuel. She let the texture of the rug beneath her feet guide her toward the desk, the building tension in her neck and shoulders loosening a little with each step away from him.

Her fingers finally connected with something rigid, and a brief flash of light illuminated a small area around her before going dark again. She picked up her cell and pressed the flashlight icon. The room glowed in the sudden brightness, tempting her to look back at the man in her bed. Instead, she sauntered into her private bathroom and closed the door.

A slow inhale and exhale calmed the uneasy feeling trying to worm its way into her thoughts. She was attracted to Dixon Mayhew. So what? She possessed enough self-control to keep from sitting on his dick and fucking him until they both found the promised land.

A mutually beneficial friends-with-benefits agreement

won't work if I don't like him. It doesn't mean I want anything more than an orgasm party once or twice a week.

His booty was definitely worth the call, and neither of them was interested in a romantic relationship. She'd leave that foolishness to Scarlet, Rose, and any other of her friends who wanted a husband or permanent boyfriend.

Thanking the universe for city-water access, she flushed and washed her hands. The woman in the mirror, who looked like she'd been banged six ways to Sunday, smirked. Even if she never rode Dixon's inspiring cock, she had his multi-talented mouth and hands—plus a boxful of toys—to entertain her until the snowstorm ended and the power was restored.

Her stomach growled as she re-entered her office, reminding her to check the time instead of checking out the man sprawled across her bed. "It's a little past noon. Are you hungry for lunch?"

He pushed up on his elbows, making the covers slip to his waist. The subtle curve of his mouth suggested he'd caught her eyeing his flexed biceps and pecs. Or he wanted to eat her again.

Heat spread through her body, despite being naked and the lack of a working furnace.

He sat up and the blankets slipped to his lap. "Food would be good, but just enough to keep up our strength. It's hard to say how long we'll be here, so we should probably ration what you have."

Hiding a grin, she crossed to the supply closet. "Would you like a jar of edible body paint? A bag of gummy boobs? Or maybe a chocolate pussy pop?"

Low chuckles filled the quiet room. "I was thinking more along the lines of a sandwich or some crackers, although I might be interested in the body paint if I can lick it off of you. What flavors do you have?"

CHAPTER FIVE

HIS HEARTBEAT STILL THUDDING IN HIS EARS, DIXON CLOSED his eyes and focused on the gentle pressure of Cerise's body covering his again. She made a damn nice blanket—before, during, and after their sexual activities. Her rough breathing caressed his neck, teasing his dick back from the land of satisfaction.

Actually, that wasn't true. He'd barely stopped himself from sliding inside her while she had wet-humped his condom-covered length. They'd both gotten off again, but only a full-blown fuck would truly satisfy him now.

He palmed her gorgeous ass and stifled a grin when she hummed against his chest. The cover of darkness was no reason to be openly smug about being eleven for eleven—or was it twelve for twelve?—on his attempts to give her an orgasm. She'd deserved at least an extra one for every time she gave him the same pleasure.

Her fingernail traced a ring around his nipple, inciting even more interest. "I'm feeling a reawakening down below. Pretty impressive recovery."

"You're an inspiring woman, and I'm making up for a lot

of years of abstinence. Besides, I can't think of a better way to pass the time than to reap the benefits of our friendship. And who knows when we'll be snowed in together again?" He groaned when she flicked her tongue across his taut peak. "What else do you have in your box of—"

Ringing echoed through the room—one, two, three, four rings—before Cerise rolled away and his sexy blanket disappeared. "Stay put until I turn on the flashlight."

A few seconds later, a beam of light reflected off the ceiling, revealing a tousled halo of silvery-blonde hair atop his breathtakingly naked lover. She stretched across the desk and her seductive voice filled the air after another ring. "Hello, BOB's Pleasure Palace. Your pleasure is important to us. How can we help you have an orgasmic day?"

Another surge of heat spread across his skin from the lust her uninhibited talk of sex prompted. She was like no other woman he'd ever known.

"Hi, Rose. Yes, Dixon's here. What happened?"

Panic ripped through him in an instant. His muscles refused to cooperate as he struggled with the tangled blankets toward the edge of the bed and finally found the rug with his bare feet.

She glanced at him, her expression changing from unease to trepidation. "Hang on a second. He's right here."

His hand shook as he took the phone from her. "My kids. Are they okay?"

Rose's brief hesitation amplified the fear. "Yes. There was an accident this morning during the senior trip, but nobody was seriously injured."

A wave of lightheadedness forced him to lean against the desk to steady himself. "What kind of accident? Was Wil hurt? I don't have the trip contact information with me. Who do I need to get in touch with? Do you have a name and a phone number?"

"A semi clipped the tour bus and it ended up in a ditch. Several of the kids got jostled and were taken to the hospital for stitches. Nothing serious enough to be admitted. They haven't released names, but the daughter of one of my employees is on the trip and she said Wil got a cut on his forehead, so he went to be checked out. The storm's supposed to let up some in about an hour, so cell signal should be back soon. I'm sure the school has tried to get in touch with you. Here's the number my employee gave me for the teacher leading their group. Mrs. Lee."

He swallowed past the tightness in his throat as he grabbed the pen and notepad by the base of the phone. "Go ahead. I'm ready."

She rattled off the number and repeated it twice. "I know I wouldn't be doing any better, but try not to worry too much. I'm sure he's okay. Can you put Cerise back on for a minute?"

"Yeah." His automatic nod made no sense since Rose couldn't see him. "Thanks. I appreciate the call. Here she is."

Cerise grasped and squeezed his forearm, her concern comforting. Then she raised the receiver to her ear. "I'm back. We're fine. Okay. I will. Thanks."

Rather than hanging up, she pressed the disconnect button and handed him the phone. After a quick hug, she nudged him toward the desk chair and gestured for him to sit.

The cool leather barely registered against his still-naked ass. Breathing through the same dread he'd experienced when Syd had crashed her bike into a tree his first summer as a single father, he punched in the string of numbers he'd written on the paper.

Let him be okay. Please let him be okay.

"Hello?"

The tentative greeting triggered more knots in his stomach. "Hello. I'm trying to reach Mrs. Lee. This is Dixon Mayhew, Wilson's dad."

"Hello, Mr. Mayhew. This is Mrs. Lee. I've heard there's been quite a storm going on today. Did you get my messages?"

He trapped the phone between his ear and his shoulder to flex the stiffness from his fingers from having gripped the phone so tightly. "No. A friend heard about the accident and called me. Is Wil okay? She said he needed stitches."

"Yes, he's going to be fine. He has six stitches on his forehead, but the doctor found no signs of concussion and assured me he can continue the trip. The chaperones and I will make sure your son follows his wound-care instructions. Would you like to talk to him? He's right here."

"Yes, please. Was anybody else hurt?"

"Just a few bumps and bruises. Nothing serious enough to disrupt the trip. Wil, your father's on the phone. Here's Wil, Mr. Mayhew."

"Thanks, Mrs. Lee." The panic receded, but adrenaline still pumped strong and hard through his body.

"Hey, Dad. No worries. Just some stitches. It looked a lot worse when I was bleeding. It was dripping all over the place. Uh, sorry. Probably shouldn't have told you that. I'm okay. Anyway, are you okay?"

A choked laugh was all he managed for a few seconds. "Blizzard, no cell service, power outage, and I got news that my kid was taken to the hospital four hundred fifty miles from home. Yeah, I'm great. Or I will be once my pulse drops to normal. Are you having a good trip, besides having your head stitched up?"

"Yep. Are you enjoying having the house to yourself?

Any hot dates?" Wil's questions conveyed the usual smirk he wore when the subject of having a parental love life came up. Thankfully, he hadn't mentioned sex.

The tension in Dixon's neck and shoulders finally loosened. "It's kind of nice not to have remind you to help with the dishes and do your laundry."

"And any dates?"

"Nope." Although he told the truth, a guilty twinge pricked at Dixon's conscience. He didn't, however, plan to share even vague details about his revived sex life with either of his children. "Busy with work."

"Aw, you should do something about that. I need to go. The new bus just got here."

"Okay. Have fun. Do what the doctors told you and listen to your chaperones."

"Of course."

"Love you, Wil."

"Love you too, Dad. See you Sunday. Oh, and go on a date."

The line went dead before he could respond, so he hung up and leaned back in the chair. Sex was one thing, but dating? He didn't need a complication like that in his life. A no-strings agreement with the woman who'd redefined sexual compatibility for him fit the bill for the foreseeable future.

"It sounds like your son survived an adventure and will have an interesting story to tell when he gets home. I'm glad he wasn't seriously injured, for both your sakes." Cerise reached for him and cast her gaze toward the bed. "Let's go back to bed. I'll give you a massage to loosen up all those tight muscles."

He clasped his hand around her smaller one and stood, relieved she hadn't shifted their time together to a discussion about Wil's accident. Talking to her was too easy, and diving back into talking about kids, divorce, and death seemed like a bad idea, too much of a couple-y thing. "There's an invitation I can't resist. Just so you know, I'm happy to return the favor. Anywhere you want."

Her coy smile assured him she wouldn't be shy about telling him exactly where to caress away the tension. "I'll definitely take you up on that."

She slipped her fingers free of his and detoured toward the closet. The curve of her incredible ass was still visible when she reached inside, inciting a shiver down his spine and through his balls. The cool air had nothing to do with the reaction.

Holding up a bottle, she grinned. "Piña colada warming massage oil. Slippery, steamy, and smells good. Edible too. Ready for a tropical fantasy?"

Her Caribbean-colored outfit from their first face-to-face meeting this morning flashed through his mind and morphed into a tiny bikini that showed off all her shapely assets.

He dropped to the bed, stretched out on his stomach, and rested his chin on his crossed arms to enjoy the view while she walked toward him. "Some sunshine would be nice, but I'm good as long as we don't get sand anywhere it doesn't belong."

PERSISTENT BUZZING PULLED DIXON FROM ANOTHER POST-orgasmic fog, but his pulse had yet to get the memo. His new friend was damn generous with the benefits, making reciprocation and one-upmanship pure enjoyment.

Cerise grunted and rolled off of him, her knee lightly brushing the top of his head. "Is that your phone or mine?"

"Both?" Careful not to pull her hair, he slid his rubbery

legs toward the edge of the bed. "My pants are over here, aren't they?"

The sheet rustled behind him and light from her cell cast the room in dim shadows. "I think so. Four calls and a dozen text messages. Don't people have better things to do during a blizzard than try to interrupt my sex life?"

He snorted as he picked up the lighter-colored item from the tangle of clothing on the rug. Something hard narrowly missed landing on his recently deflated dick. A vibration hummed through his upper thigh. "Fifteen calls and thirty-two texts. Evidently, people think my sex life needs more interrupting than yours."

Her uninhibited laughter assured him she didn't give a damn about who got the shorter stick. Life wasn't a fucking contest, like Teri had always tried to make it.

Then the lights flickered on, nearly blinding him. A low hum suggested the heating system had kicked on, but disappointment warred with relief.

She raised her eyebrows at him. "Why the frown? The sex-fest is far from over. We're trapped here until the roads are plowed."

"Good point. I kind of liked using my other senses to learn your body, although watching your face while you come is pretty damn rewarding." A quick scroll through his missed calls, voicemails, and messages yielded only two needing responses. He also had to inform his ex about Wil's accident before she heard about it secondhand and accused him of trying to keep her from knowing what was going on with their kids, as if she couldn't call and talk to them herself. As he scrolled through his contacts, his phone vibrated in his hand and her name popped up on the screen. "Damn it."

"Problem?" Cerise's concerned tone proved she was nothing like his former wife.

"You could say that. I have to take this call." Resting his elbows on his knees, he tapped the Answer icon and lifted his cell to his ear. "Dixon Mayhew."

Teri huffed out her usual disgruntled growl. "Why do you do that? You know it's me calling, but you act like you don't, like I'm just one of your customers."

He rolled his eyes and resisted waving his arm for her to get on with the reason she'd called—to chew his ass out for something he had no control over. Any second, she would launch into a tirade without any prompting from him.

"I've been trying to reach you for hours. Why was your phone turned off?"

"It wasn't." *Interpret that any way you want to. You're going to anyway.*

"You were avoiding my calls? That's so childish, Dixon. Speaking of children, you need to speak to Sydney and Wilson. I'm traveling to France on business in June and I want them to go with me. They told me they can't go."

Can you blame them? You're not exactly mother-of-the-year material. "She has a mandatory internship and he's working all summer to save money for college. They're being responsible, and I'm not forcing them to give that up for a vacation. Besides, she's an adult and he will be in a week. If they choose not go, that's their business. It isn't my decision. Or yours."

The high-pitched squeak on the other end of the line warned him the outburst had only begun. How had he survived fourteen years of selfish behavior and endless rants?

At least she hasn't heard about the accident yet. "I got a call earlier from Mrs. Lee, the teacher leading the senior trip."

"That's next week, isn't it?"

"This week. They're in New York City right now. There was a traffic accident and Wil had to get stitches." Holding his breath, he waited for inevitable accusations and condemnation.

Better to let her blow off steam.

"Why didn't anyone call me? You didn't put me on the emergency contact form, did you? We agreed to shared parenting. You always try to exclude me. Say something!"

He exhaled, so tired of dealing with her self-centered bullshit. *Time to nip this nonsense in the bud.* "You told me you were going to be out of the country, so I put my sister as the secondary contact number. By the way, Wil is fine. Six stitches in his forehead. I talked to him and the teacher. The doctors say he can finish the trip. No one else was seriously injured, either."

"That meeting was postponed."

His snarky insinuation had clearly gone right over her head as usual. Why did he waste his breath? "I have to go."

"Fine. But I expect you to…"

He closed his eyes, hoping she ran out of steam soon, but the line went silent. A quick glance at the screen showed the call had ended.

Thank god for small favors.

He dropped his phone onto the bed beside him and questioned his sanity for the millionth time since the divorce. What had he ever seen in the woman?

"Wow. Your ex is a piece of work, isn't she?" The bed shifted behind him and then Cerise's fingers caressed the tight muscles in his neck, sending the tension southward. "I couldn't help but overhear the banshee screeching."

Embarrassment tried to creep in, but anger still outweighed it. "She doesn't give a damn that our son could've been hurt a lot worse or that he and our daughter would rather stay home and work than spend a month in Europe entertaining themselves while she's busy with clients.

It's always about her. And here I am, feeling guilty because I didn't have cell signal during a snowstorm while my kid was having his head stitched up."

"You're a good father. Don't ever let her convince you otherwise." Her breath feathered along his upper back as her hands worked his shoulders. "Want to watch me give you a blow job? Unless you have more messages to deal with, of course."

CHAPTER SIX

"HOW MANY ORGASMS DID YOU GIVE AND RECEIVE WHILE you were snowed in with Dixon?"

Cerise swirled the purplish liquid in her glass and downed another swallow to delay answering Rose Holloway's truth-or-dare question.

Honestly? Too many to count. I blew his mind and he blew mine.

Why didn't she say that thought out loud to her friends like she normally would?

Poppy Gardner grinned behind her blackberry bramble. "That many, huh? Details, woman. I need details."

Snickers and snorts filled the living room, not surprising since all five of her menopausal or nearly menopausal friends had found time in their busy schedules for the first of their twice weekly dinner, drinks, and dish nights. They expected plenty of D tonight—dishing, not the dick kind—although Rose and Scarlet Brinks-Whitaker, the only two of the group who were married, would more than likely get laid when they went home. Poppy, Sienna, and Carnie were still among the single-and-happy women getting the real D vicariously through marital stories and Cerise's exploits from her twenties, thirties, and forties.

Carnie stood at the bar with the ingredients for another batch of brambles set out in front of her. Her bartending skills had most definitely improved over the last several weeks. "Who needs a refill before we hear all about power-outage sex?"

Raising her empty glass, Cerise silently thanked the universe for the slight reprieve. "These are really good. Your mixology classes must be going well."

The owner of The Ringer Saloon nodded as she measured two shots of gin into the ice-filled shaker. "It's been a lot of fun. I'm almost ready to hop behind the bar to fill in when I need to. That should make things easier than calling in an employee if somebody has an emergency. Nice attempt to change the subject, by the way."

"I'm not changing the subject. Just figuring out how to tally them. Are we counting masturbation too?"

The clink of the shot glass against the bar joined a round of hoots and laughter, her shock-effect statement earning more reaction from the gathering than it would've gotten from Dixon.

Scarlet's grin widened as she joined Carnie. "Of course. Nelson loves watching me play with my vibrator, but don't tell him I told you. He's still a little uncomfortable with me discussing our sex adventures with all of you. Good thing he isn't that uptight when it's happening."

Gathering her red hair into a messy bun on top of her head, Poppy pinned Cerise with a hard stare. "Numbers, blondie. If you can remember how many times you got off by oral, vaginal, and other means with a guy from college, you can remember the details of a ten-hour hookup that happened five days ago."

"It was fourteen hours." Holding out her glass for a refill, Cerise willed away the heat creeping up her neck. When in her life had she ever been hesitant to share specifics about her sexual encounters? "Eleven given and twenty-two received."

Other than the hum of the refrigerator in the adjoining room, silence filled the space for the count of six—a full second for each person in the room. Then gasps and exclamations broke the rare quiet.

"Line up, ladies!" Carnie hoisted the shaker, rattling ice against metal. "This calls for a toast!"

Sienna grabbed Cerise's hand, pulling her up from one of the overstuffed armchairs and dragging her to the bar. "Any woman who can still walk, talk, and think after that many orgasms deserves the first refill. Holy hell, I wouldn't even remember my name, let alone how many times I came. Damn, that has to be a world record or something."

With her palm cupped over her crotch, Rose winced. "No kidding. I'd be lucky to survive half that. Seriously though, give me quality over quantity any day. How good could they be?"

Damn good. Excellent. The best I've ever had.

Cerise climbed onto the barstool. "It doesn't have to be either-or if your partner knows what he's doing."

Her bartending friend poured a generous helping of bramble into her glass. "Does Dixon have a brother or a cousin? I need some of that."

"How would I know? It wasn't exactly a get-to-know-you date." A gulp of her cocktail inspired a frown, but Carnie's facial expression was the least of Cerise's concerns. Couldn't she have made the drink stronger? "Don't you have a bar full of men to choose from?"

Their bartender shuddered. "Oh, you mean self-aggrandizing flirts like Simon Cortez? I'll pass. He probably doesn't know a vagina from a hole in the wall."

Rose snickered and bumped shoulders with Poppy. "Or he might actually know his way around a woman's body. You never can tell."

Poppy's cheeks flushed a ruddy shade of pink, sparking Cerise's curiosity. Had her redheaded friend bumped body parts with the owner of Cortez Homebuilders?

Ducking her head, Poppy fussed with the hem of her sweatshirt. "Can we talk about something other than sex? You know, since half of us aren't getting any and haven't for… Never mind how long."

"Yeah, well, I didn't get any of the real thing, either." Cerise's muttered admission clearly wasn't muttered enough since a hush fell again and all eyes jerked toward her. "What?"

Sienna perched a hand on her hip and her midnight-black eyebrows dipped low. "You're telling us you shared thirty-three orgasms with the tech wizard and you didn't have sex? Like actual *intercourse*?"

"Yep." She shrugged. "I agree with Poppy. Let's talk about something else. I'm starting an online store in May. BUBs & BUGs. Or maybe BOBs & BOGs. I haven't decided yet."

"Sounds like outdoor stuff." The look on Poppy's face matched the relief in Cerise's mind. "Camping and hiking gear?"

"Uh, no. BUBs. Backup boyfriends. BUGs. Backup girlfriends. BOGs. Battery-operated girlfriends. BOB's Pleasure Palace focuses mostly on the wants and needs of women and LGBTQ folks. People of every gender should be able to buy the right tools." Maybe talking about creating a cyber boutique wasn't such a great idea after all. *All sex. All the time.* "I'm hungry. What kind of soup did you bring, Rose?"

"Chicken with homemade noodles. Meg was home for spring break this past week and she made all kinds of good stuff. Noodles, cookies, two pies, enough lasagna to feed an army. I think she misses having a kitchen in the dorm, and she likes making sure Barton and I have some easy meals after working at the lumberyard all day." Rose hooked her arm through Poppy's and walked into the kitchen. "How are the new hires working out? Everything going smoothly with the big contract?"

Laughter from across the room drowned out Poppy's response, but her frown suggested her housecleaning business had hit a snag or two recently. Without question, she'd obviously engaged in a hookup with Simon. Was he making her uncomfortable since he'd contracted Clean As A Whistle to ready all his new houses for showings and closings after construction was complete?

Since Poppy clearly didn't want to discuss the situation between her and Cortez, Cerise focused on playing hostess. She had plenty of experience, having been the charming trophy wife who'd entertained her late husbands' business associates and economic equals. Her combination of brains, physical beauty, and self-confidence had beguiled the men, chafed the women, and garnered more propositions than she could shake a dick at. Finding true friends in Scarlet, Rose, Poppy, Sienna, and Carnie was a gift she would never take for granted.

One by one, they sat at the glass-topped dining table, their happy chatter lightening her mood.

Poppy nudged Cerise's elbow. "You okay? You're awfully tight-lipped tonight. I'm glad to listen if you want to talk."

Her attention still on a chunk of vodka-soaked mango on her fork, Cerise shrugged. “Menopause and tired of winter.”

Lowering her voice another notch, the usually happy-go-lucky redhead leaned closer. “Can we chat later? In private? I need some advice.”

“What are you two whispering about over there?”

Scarlet’s question cut short Cerise’s attempt to answer, so she gave Poppy a subtle nod. “We were trying to decide what to give you for your birthday next month.”

“How about that new role-playing game you told me about on the phone yesterday? Sounds like fun.” The former NASA engineer waggled her eyebrows. “Maybe I can convince Nelson to dress up like Viking warrior and plunder me with his sword.”

The comment drew eye-rolls from the single women at the table, but at least it redirected the conversation again. By nine o’clock, a date had been set for Scarlet’s birthday get-together and a dozen or more gift ideas tossed around. They’d switched to hot chocolate and tea partway through the planning since everybody had to drive home tonight and go to work bright and early tomorrow morning.

Poppy hung back when Cerise walked the others to the foyer to say goodnight, a sure sign whatever was going on with her biggest client required immediate attention. Her redheaded friend sank into the couch as soon as the front door closed. “I think I’m going to have to break my contract with Cortez Homebuilders.”

Cerise frowned as she sat in the adjacent armchair, tucking her legs under her. “Is Simon complaining about your work? Or is he doing something to make you feel unsafe or awkward? Because I’m more than happy to take care of that problem.”

Poppy’s drawn-out sigh warned her the situation was

more complicated than it seemed. “So…yeah. Remember when I was a bridesmaid in my cousin’s wedding two years ago?”

Molten hormones blasted through Cerise’s pores, immersing her in a cloud of suffocating heat. She tugged her sweater over her head and tossed it on the floor. Then she took a giant swig of ice water from the insulated bottle on the end table, wishing she could dump the contents over her head. “Holy hell. Kilauea is erupting again. Yes, I remember. Some bubble-gum pink monstrosity with cotton-candy fluffs on the skirt. I hope you burned that thing.”

Her friend didn’t laugh. “The day I got home. Anyway, Simon was there. He and the groom know each other from college, I think. We were both a little tipsy by the end of the reception from all the champagne. And when he offered to escort me to my suite, our mouths decided kissing in the hotel elevator would be cool, and we sort of hooked up. On the couch. In the shower. In bed. All night.”

Rather than claiming bragging rights for guessing the truth, Cerise simply nodded. Consensual sex was a no-judgment zone.

Dragging her hands through her hair, Poppy grimaced. Half her messy bun escaped the pony tail holder from the motion. Instead of repairing the damage, she slipped the elastic band around her wrist and combed her fingers through the long red strands. “It was the best sex I’ve ever had, but we agreed it was a one-time thing in the morning. No harm. No foul. Back to being acquaintances and business associates. And it’s worked out fine. Our interactions haven’t been awkward at all. He emails me when he needs to schedule a cleaning and I send someone out. Completely professional. Until last week.”

A surge of protectiveness set off Cerise's fiery temper. "What happened? Did he threaten to—"

"No." Poppy shook her head. "He knows I won't put up with that shit from any of my clients, whether it's me or one of my employees at the job site. Anyway, I've been doing all the cleaning over at the new development since Lizzie went on maternity leave three weeks ago and Grace hurt her wrist while she was shoveling snow not long after. Being down two of my best cleaners means I've been working a bunch of extra hours to get everything done on time. On Wednesday, Simon saw the house I was cleaning was still lit up on his way home and stopped by to turn off the lights and make sure he didn't have a squatter, not knowing I was there. He just about gave me a heart attack when he walked in the kitchen with a baseball bat. And, well, one thing led to another. Again."

A chill settled over Cerise's bare arms as the latest hot flash dissipated. "I hope the sex was at least as good as the first time."

The instantaneous flames on Poppy's cheeks confirmed it had met—or, more likely, exceeded—her expectations, but the problem seemed to be more than a repeat hookup. "Better. Then he showed up Thursday evening at the next house on the list. And Friday and yesterday."

"And you two christened all those as well?" A tiny stab of jealousy poked at her unsatisfied libido, especially given that Dixon hadn't made any attempt to set up their next FWB session yet.

"Yep." Her friend plopped sideways on the couch, burying her face behind a red-haired waterfall. "He claims he wants to date me, but you've seen the way he flirts with every woman he sees. I know it'll end badly. My relationships with men always do. I'll fall in love and he'll fall into the habit of lying and cheating."

"You're asking the wrong person for advice about romantic stuff. After waking up with two dead husbands, I'll be sleeping alone for the rest of my life. Except for my toys. They can be recharged or the batteries can be replaced." Goose bumps had spread over her arms, but chilling in a camisole beat having to remove her sweater again before she headed to bed. "No sleepovers for me."

"Didn't you nap while you were snowbound with Dixon? I mean, twenty-two orgasms in fourteen hours is a lot. I can't imagine not resting in between." Poppy peeked out from her hair with a thoughtful expression. "Did you fold out the bed? I think my body would revolt if I engaged in everything but intercourse multiple times in a row on a couch or a chair."

"No, I didn't nap." A cold sweat spread across her chest and neck, but it wasn't from a hot flash. Remembering his mouth on her breasts and between her thighs sparked sexual instead of hormonal heat. "My hips and lower back wouldn't have survived without the bed. I think he fell asleep twice. I closed my eyes and meditated."

"Hm." Poppy glanced at her from her reclining position. "Are you planning to have actual sex with him? Or is he a one-and-done? Not that it's any of my business. I'm just thinking if you can kick him to the curb, I can do the same with Simon."

Cerise shrugged off the question and the twinge of disappointment the probable answer sparked. "I don't know. Maybe. He asked if I'd be interested in a friends-with-benefits hookup one or twice a week, but I haven't heard from him since we parted ways Tuesday night. I'm sure as hell not calling or texting him unless it's about installing the new security system here at the house. He knows I'm willing. It's on him to make arrangements if he wants to follow through.

That said, he better not wait too long or the answer will be no."

CHAPTER SEVEN

DIXON EMPTIED THE CARAFE INTO HIS TRAVEL MUG AND screwed on the lid as Wil scarfed down a stack of pancakes swimming in syrup. "Don't forget the appointment at three to get your stitches taken out. I'll meet you at the clinic a few minutes before. Any ideas for your birthday supper tonight? Syd's making a cake."

"Did I hear my name?" Clad in the fuzzy robe and matching slippers he'd given her for Christmas three months ago, his daughter shuffled into the kitchen. She paused for a giant yawn at the fridge before pulling out the orange juice and the rest of the leftover pancakes from the batch she'd made yesterday morning. Her spring break visit meant upping his willpower to avoid all the extra carbs she would lure his stomach with all week.

Her brother looked up from his breakfast and grinned. "Yep. You're making me a blueberry poke cake. Dad's taking us to The Vinery for supper. Gotta have their ribs."

She snorted and moved to the toaster. "You're so predictable. Full rack. Dry rub. Sweet potato fries and coleslaw. The blueberries are already defrosting. I got them out of the freezer last night."

"Predictable is good. No need to adjust your expectations." Wil swirled the last forkful in the remaining sticky puddle and stuffed it in his mouth. "Mmm."

His son's comments made Dixon's chest squeeze. Teri would likely forget what day it was—again—and claim she was in meetings all day, thereby excusing her lack of having ten seconds to acknowledge her kid's milestone eighteenth birthday.

Whatever.

Instead of dwelling on her shortcomings, he checked his pants pocket for his phone, slipped on his coat, and shouldered his computer bag. "I need to get going. Early install. Eight minutes until you need to leave for school."

Wil pushed away from the table, his dishes in hand. "Try not to get snowed in again."

Heat crept up Dixon's neck, but he let out a low chuckle as he gave his son a one-armed hug. "Already checked the forecast. No blizzard. Not even flurries. That's why you're driving instead of me taking you. Happy birthday."

A loud bark of laughter echoed through the kitchen, a reminder that Wil had inherited his—and not Teri's—sense of humor. "Thanks, Dad."

After a quick stop to drop a kiss on the top of Syd's head, he headed to the door. "See you this afternoon. I should be home a little after four. Call or text if you need anything."

"We need you to go on a date."

The request came in stereo as he stepped into the garage. He shook his head in lieu of answering and shut the kitchen door. After a week of mulling over the mind-blowing day he'd spent with Cerise, he still couldn't muster the courage or the will to engage in more than a physical relationship with her. If anything could've convinced to give romance a second chance, the lethal combination of her beauty, her intelligence, her sense of humor, her honesty, and their sexual chemistry should've done it.

And her willingness to skip the risks of commitment.

She was so damn perfect for him, but he'd been too chicken to call or even text to set up their next adventure, let alone consider dating her.

As he drove to his first appointment, his mind wandered off into the memories of those fourteen hours—the same ones that had kept him company every night when he went to bed, every morning in the shower, and at random times while he was working, eating, talking to a customer, and everything else for the last seven days. She practically lived in his brain.

Eventually, he would have to contact her to schedule the revamp of her home security system. Or she might decide to hire somebody else since he'd pretty much ghosted her, other than sending an invoice for the BOB's Pleasure Palace job.

Stop being a coward and just touch base with her now.

He tapped the Bluetooth button on his steering wheel and waited for the prompt for a command. "Call Cerise Wethers."

His pulse thumped in his ears while the call connected and ramped up with each successive ring. Seven rings became eight and eight rings became nine, which meant he would probably have to leave a voicemail message.

With his finger hovering over the End Call button, she finally picked up. "Cerise Wethers."

A chill shivered up his spine at her standoffish greeting and lack of a friendly hello since he was in her contacts and she had to know he was the caller. "Hi, it's Dixon. Do you have a few minutes to talk?"

"One. I'm in a breakfast meeting." If a tone of voice could say go fuck yourself, hers would be it.

Determined to make amends for disappearing on her, he took a deep breath and dove in. "First, I apologize for not calling or texting sooner. The reasons don't matter. It was inconsiderate. Second, I'd like to put the security system update for your house on the schedule for next week if that works for you. We can do the interior whatever day is convenient for you. If you're okay with us being outside when you're not home, we'll finish the exterior by the end of the week. Third, I owe you at least four orgasms, if you're still interested. Tell me when and where, and I'll make time to take care of—"

"Eleven seconds."

"—your needs. I'd love to eat your pussy for lunch and fuck you 'til you scream. I bought an economy pack of condoms for the occasion." A long silence followed his rundown, leaving him to wonder if she'd punched the red End button. His navigation screen showed they were still connected, and the possibility of her hanging up on him for using raunchy language was negligible at best. That didn't, however, calm the churning in his gut.

"I've added it to my calendar and can meet at twelve thirty today to iron out the details if you're available then."

Her vague wording suggested she didn't want whoever was in the room with her to know who she was talking to or why—something he truly appreciated for the sake of their privacy.

He flipped on his turn signal and slowed for the upcoming traffic light. "Twelve thirty is good for me. The shop? Your house?"

"The latter. See you then."

Before he could confirm the location, the call dropped, telling him she was done with their conversation.

At least she'd agreed to see him and he hadn't carried the

box of condoms into the house after a stop at the store on his birthday. It was hidden under his seat—one of the few places no one was likely to find it. Asking Wil for a strip from his supply would mark the end of Dixon's private sex life and too much knowledge about his son's extracurricular activities.

Following the winding road to the newest Cortez Homebuilders development, he forced his thoughts to the upgrade a dozen of the contracted buyers had requested. Rodney had installed the basic hardwired system in every unit during the construction phase, so the addition of smart home features would go quickly, while also occupying Dixon's mind until his lunch date.

Right. Like working twelve-hour days the last week has made any difference.

He parked along the curb in front of the first house on his list, glad to see Simon's truck already there. A layer of gravel marked where the concrete driveway would be poured as soon as the weather cooperated.

As he grabbed his tool bag and an upgrade kit, the unmistakable sound of a car door closing echoed through the chilly air. His client stalked toward him, looking like he'd gotten news that the new-housing market had collapsed. "Hey, Simon. Problem with the add-on installs this morning?"

The other man stopped a few feet away and extended his arm. "Morning, Dixon. Woman troubles. Can't live with 'em. Can't live without 'em. Ready to get started?"

Dixon shook Simon's hand and sighed. "I hear you. Ready when you are."

They walked together to the entry pad on the front porch and Dixon punched in the access code. The light turned green as an audible click signaled the locks disengaging. He handed his long-time customer a pair of slip-on booties for his shoes and opened the door.

When they'd both covered their boots to protect the floors, Simon stepped inside. "You've been married before. What makes women tick?"

Dixon's loud snort filled the entryway. "I'm divorced. There's a reason for that. Multiple reasons, actually. Among them is my complete and utter inability to understand how women's minds work. I didn't know you were dating somebody. Pretty sure word about that would spread like wildfire, considering your reputation as a guy who flirts with anything in a skirt. Or short shorts. Or tight jeans. A garbage bag. Without a Y chromosome."

His friend's eyebrows dipped toward his nose and a frown creased his shaven face. "I like women. Just because I enjoy talking to them, it doesn't mean I'm trying to pick them up. Besides, maybe I'm wife shopping."

"You? Wife shopping?" Heading for the kitchen, Dixon tried to wrap his brain around that possibility. *Impossibility?* "So you met your soul mate? And she won't give you the time of day?"

A noisy huff spoke volumes about Simon's comfort level. "It's been two years and I can't get her out of my system. We've hooked up multiple times recently, but she won't go out on a date with me. I'm guessing my reputation has something to do with it, even though I'm not the manwhore people seem to think I am. I haven't slept with another woman since she and I got together the first time. Hell, I haven't even dated anyone else. What am I supposed to do?"

"You're asking the wrong guy." Dixon set his tools and supplies on the center island and pinned Simon with a sympathetic stare. "My marriage was hell. The only good thing to come out of it was my kids, and I'm surprised they're normal and well-adjusted."

"Because you're a decent dad." Shaking his head, the

builder pulled his humming phone from his coat pocket. He frowned as he glanced at the screen. "I need to take this call. I'll leave the shoe covers by the front door. Let's get together for a beer sometime soon."

Giving a nod, Dixon picked up the kit he needed to install and got to work laying out its contents. "Sounds good. Shoot me a text."

Simon's thumbs-up accompanied his exit and then his greeting carried through the unfurnished space. "Cortez Homebuilders. Simon Cortez."

A few more business-sounding bits of conversation faded to nothing when the front door clunked shut, making Dixon glad most of his contact with customers happened through email.

As he completed the seventh of twelve upgrades, his cell belted out an alarm, reminding him of his lunch appointment—not that he or his dick would ever forget the opportunity to spend some naked time with his friend with unmatched benefits. The exercise should relieve the tension that had been building during his self-imposed break after their snowed-in sexfest.

By the time he tapped in the security code she'd texted him at her gated driveway, his pulse was thumping through his erection and he was about to crawl out of his skin from the need to touch, lick, and kiss every inch of her body into orgasmic submission. If she agreed to actual intercourse, he hoped he lasted more than a few minutes.

The gate slid closed behind him and he followed the cleared pavement to the house he'd only seen in blueprints and from above in the aerial photos she'd provided for his bid on the home-security update project. As he rounded the final curve, the impressive brick-and-glass structure came into view. A three-car garage with space outside to park at least a dozen vehicles took up the entire lower side of the residence, but he turned toward the loop that seemed to be a guest drop-off and pick-up area at the steps to the double front doors. The property looked like it was built for hosting lavish parties and entertaining people a whole lot wealthier than he was.

He stopped a few car-lengths past the stairs, shut off the engine, and rummaged under the seat for his secret stash. Three foil packets would certainly last the hour he'd scheduled for their lunch meeting. Whether or not she allowed him to stay that long remained to be seen, but he chose optimism over doubt. Being a monk for the rest of his life would suck —and not in the good way.

As he approached what was obviously the main entrance, the left side of the double doors swung open, despite his arrival at twelve twenty-three. Cerise stepped forward, form-fitting pants and heels making her legs look a mile long and a sweater hugging her incredible breasts. Her hair ruffled in the light breeze and the sunlight caught the sparkling silvery strands.

She leaned her shoulder against the doorjamb, looking far more relaxed than he felt, even though one of her eyebrows arched toward her forehead. "You're seven minutes early."

Mustering the wherewithal to match wits with her, he shrugged as he closed the distance between them. "Time enough to give you an extra apology orgasm. Five instead of four. You have a supply of toys here, don't you? I'm ready to get started with my groveling."

Those amazing lips twitched, like she was trying not to laugh at his bribery attempt to keep her from kicking his ass to the curb. Then she crooked her finger at him and pivoted on the sexy pink shoes that matched her lipstick and a vibrator she'd used on herself while he watched last week. Without waiting for him, she headed inside.

The gentle sway of her hips pulled him into the high-ceilinged entryway. He shoved the door closed and trailed her across the polished hardwood floor. They passed a huge formal great room, an equally fancy dining room, and a cave-like library with a stone fireplace before arriving in a more casual living area. A pair of comfortable-looking couches and four oversized armchairs formed a large but welcoming square around a low glass-and-iron table, hinting it was used for get-togethers with friends or family. No wall separated it from a spacious kitchen more suited to chatting with guests than serving a seven-course dinner.

She pointed toward the closest sofa when she detoured toward the granite counter with bar-stool seating for four. "Have a seat. Are you hungry?"

"Not for food at the moment." He shrugged out of his coat, removed his shoes, and dropped onto the middle cushion. "But feel free to eat lunch while I eat you."

Instead of answering, she retrieved a tote and a carryout bag with the local deli's name on it from the end of countertop. "If you don't need sustenance at some point over the next hour and six minutes, you're not working hard enough. Turkey club on sourdough okay?"

His traitorous stomach rumbled, but his cock would've growled louder if it could make noise. "Perfect. After I have an appetizer or two. Are you undressing yourself? Or do I get that honor?"

CHAPTER EIGHT

THE RAGING LUST IN DIXON'S GAZE SENT SHIVERS ALONG HER spine, but Cerise maintained her unhurried pace to the cozy sitting area and set their lunch and her bag of goodies on the glass-top center table. Instead of sitting beside him or answering his question about who got to remove her clothing, she unfastened the side button and zipper of her wool trousers and let them puddle around her ankles. Her feet easily slid free of her shoes and pants so she could perch her right foot on the couch next to his knee.

A wicked grin let her know when he spotted the words on the front of the cheeky panties she'd chosen to put on after his call and breakfast with her financial advisor. He feathered his palm up her inner thigh to the lettering across her public bone. Then he slipped past the leg hole and through her slick folds. "Slippery when wet. I can confirm you're both slippery and wet."

She barely stayed upright when he circled her clit, only saving herself by grabbing onto his shoulders with both hands. Her brain cells fell victim to the distraction, rendering her speechless, but a breathy moan escaped.

He dipped his calloused finger inside her before raising it to his mouth and licking it clean. “Mm. You taste so good. Are you thinking about me eating your pussy and fucking you until you scream?”

While she wasn’t about to admit to replaying their snowed-in activities dozens of times in her mind over the last week, she couldn’t deny the truth in the moment. A slight adjustment to her stance brought his face even with her hips. She arched toward him as she urged him forward with a tug of his shirt. “I think the answer to that question is obvious. Are you?”

“Every damn minute of the last week. Get ready for orgasm number one.” He buried his face in her crotch and worked his hands under her sweater to her breasts. The brush of his thumbs across her nipples amplified the tremors rippling through her body. Then he sucked her clit between his lips, not bothering to move her panties out of the way.

Friction from his tongue against the damp fabric covering her bundle of nerves joined the sensations buzzing from her taut nipples to her very core. Lightheadedness forced her to tighten her hold on him as he added licking to the action. Within seconds, a hoarse cry scrambled up her throat and echoed in her ears.

Without a moment’s hesitation, he released her clit and plunged two fingers into her vagina, curving into the spot he’d become an expert at finding during their adventures in the dark. “So wet and slippery. Squeeze me. Let me feel you come again. Then I want to fuck you from behind so I can see and feel your spectacular ass.”

The thought that he’d embraced the blunt talk she enjoyed during sex flitted through her consciousness and disappeared with his rhythmic thrusts and the feeling winding tighter and tighter again.

She gasped with each deep stroke to her G-spot. "Fuck, fuck, fuck, fuck, fuck."

"Not until I give you orgasm number two." His raspy voice triggered goose bumps up her arms and across her back. "Come, Cerise. Now, so I can fuck you."

His words sent her flying again, but his persistent in-and-out glide made her soar, drawing out her pleasure for what seemed like forever.

Drowning in sexual bliss, she doubled over as her muscles failed her. Thankfully, he caught her in a fireman's hold and draped her across the arm of the overstuffed couch. Her eyes drifted shut while she fought to catch her breath.

"That was so damn sexy." Rustling and the *scritch-scritch-scritch* of a zipper sounded beside her, the distinctive tear of a foil packet following soon after. His warm palms pushed her underwear past her hips, to her knees, and down her calves, revving her pulse before it recovered from rounds one and two. "Are you ready for more? Or do you need a minute?"

She blinked at him over her shoulder, surprised he was willing to delay his own gratification, if only for a few seconds. "The rest of our clothes…need to go first."

"Yours maybe, but I'm not wasting time getting naked just yet." He eased her sweater up and freed her from it in a gentle motion that showed far more restraint than she expected. Her bra landed on the floor a moment later. "Better."

His defensive tone suggested he didn't possess as much control over his body as he would've liked. She could hardly fault him for wanting to last more than a minute or two after eight years without sex.

Instead of verbally sparring with him, which was a special kind of foreplay of its own, she wiggled her butt at him.

Spasms still shuddered through her lower belly, but anticipation made her entire body ache for his welcome invasion. "Ready and getting impatient."

The brush of his work pants against her bare skin triggered a tremor in dozens of nerve endings, but she bit her lip to hold in an order to fuck her now or leave. She absolutely wanted him to break her dry spell.

"Hard and fast or slow and easy?" His humid breath heated her shoulder blades with his husky question. Then he licked a path up her spine as he nudged the head of his dick into her still-pulsing vagina. He inched a bit deeper before pausing. "Jesus, you feel amazing."

Her muscles pulled him a little farther inside her, causing her breath to hitch. "Give me your cock. All of it. Hard and fast."

His immediate thrust shoved her against the padded arm of the couch, but the high of being completely filled by him shot her toward the stars again. He hammered into her over and over, driving her far beyond any pleasure she'd experienced in her life and setting off wave after wave of unending ecstasy. The scream she was pretty originated from her pussy mingled with a throaty masculine bellow. Her entire body shook, even when he sprawled on top of her, pinning her down and keeping her afloat.

Her pulse thumped in her ears in time with the rapid panting against her hair for several minutes. She'd had a lot of good and really good sex over the years, but getting nailed by a someone whose P seemed made to fit her V to a T and gave more than he got was an anomaly. Would he possibly agree to a long-term friends-with-benefits arrangement?

"Holy fuck." He levered up for a second before returning to his previous position. His heat seeped into her pores everywhere his skin made contact with hers. "I hope I'm not squishing you, because I don't think I can move yet."

His weight grounded her, feeling truly perfect after her out-of-body experience with him. "Uh-uh. Nice."

He grunted and shifted off of her. "Nice? Not exactly what I was going for."

Instantly missing his presence, she shimmied free instead of trying to stop him from pulling away. "I meant it as a compliment. Hungry for lunch now?"

"Huh. Bathroom first."

When she pointed toward the closest bath down the hall from the upper-level entertainment area, his footsteps faded. A door clicked shut, leaving her alone to work her public persona into place again.

Long-term? Not if I can help it.

She sat up to test her equilibrium before meandering to the sink for a washcloth. Between her leaking vaginal fluids, his saliva, and the lube from the condom, her inner thighs were stickier than a freshly licked lolli-cock from BOB's. After a thorough rinse, she turned off the water and hung the wet cloth on the towel rack.

"Two more orgasms to go, not that I'm not up for more if you are."

Somehow he'd managed to sneak up on her, but nearly a decade of people trying to get a rise out of her with snide comments kept her from reacting. She pivoted toward him and shrugged. "We'll see. What would you like to drink? Water? Coffee? I have decaf and regular. Tea? I'm guessing not wine since you probably have more business appointments this afternoon."

"Booked until four." His gaze dropped from her eyes to parts a little farther south and up again. Appreciation came in the form of another slower assessment. "Decaf's good, but I can make it if you tell me where to find everything."

She walked her fingers down the column of buttons leading to the erection already reforming behind his zipper. Not pausing, she continued past the waistband. "You can have coffee if you take off your clothes."

He sucked in a breath and grinned.

After a firm press of her palm against the growing lump, she swiveled toward the sink for a glass of water. "You think I'm joking? I'm not. I know you're not shy about being naked with me, so lose the shirt, pants, and everything else you're wearing."

A button pinged against the slate floor and bounced under the refrigerator in his haste to undress. His belt and khakis landed on top of his TMI oxford shirt, followed by his socks and boxer briefs. "I hope we're not going to be interrupted by a butler, housekeeper, or gardener."

She chuckled at his flushed cheeks and unnecessary paranoia about getting caught in the act. "Only if they show up on the wrong days. Coffee and the cold press machine are in the appliance garage."

Proving he wasn't inept or deliberately helpless, he made coffee with the same kind of press he said he had at home and then joined her on the couch for lunch, some surprisingly comfortable conversation, and a cowgirl ride that included three more orgasms for her and one doozy for him. Their easy rapport should've been a huge warning sign, but he didn't want a relationship any more than she did.

Besides, I know how to recognize when the line blurs and it's time to end the benefits.

After another trip to the bathroom down the hall to make sure he was presentable enough to head to his next upgrade location, Dixon stood at the front door with Cerise. Her face was beautifully flushed from their activities, suggesting she wouldn't be opposed to hooking up again.

He zipped his coat and fished his keyring from his pocket. "Are you free Friday night? Maybe about six thirty? My kids are hanging out with friends, so I'll have a couple hours free."

She caught his gaze in a lengthy stare, like she was evaluating his performance and whether or not she wanted to be available. "I need to check my calendar. I'll let you know later today."

With a nod, he opened the door to leave. What the hell did a guy say to the woman he was having sex with but not dating? "This was…"

No, not nice.

Just what I needed?

Pretty fucking amazing?

Would a kiss cross the invisible line they'd drawn in the sheets?

He raised his hand to wave goodbye in lieu of finding out. "Worth repeating. Don't you think?"

Her blonde eyebrows rose and a smirk curved her sexy mouth. "Yes. See you soon."

He nodded once more, stepped outside, and sorted through his keys to stop himself from looking over his shoulder at her. "Soon."

"Oh, and Dixon? I think you should aim for six next time." The door snicked shut behind him.

A chuckle snuck out as he descended to the loop where he'd parked.

How about seven?

Watching her bliss out from his just-like-riding-a-bike skills was damn rewarding. His own satisfaction was a bonus.

The afternoon passed quickly with the repetitive installation tasks that let his mind wander to the best sex he could remember and his body still humming from having his dick inside a woman for the first time in eight years. Hell, it had been better than any fantasy he'd ever conjured.

At a minute after four, he toed off his shoes and set his computer bag at his feet to take off his coat and hang it in the hall closet. Then he followed the low hum of conversation to the kitchen. As he entered the room, his kids clammed up, warning him they'd probably been talking about his social life—or, according to them, the lack thereof—for the umpteenth time. "Hey. Happy birthday again, Wil. What's going on?"

"Thanks, Dad. Not much." Fiddling with the cell phone in his hand, his son shrugged.

Syd rested her elbows on the breakfast bar, her bright smile not fooling him for a second. "Cake is done and I went to the store for ice cream. We were talking about Wil's adventure last week. My senior trip wasn't nearly as exciting. Did you have a good day at work? Do anything interesting?"

Ignoring the bait, Dixon aimed straight for the stack of mail on the counter and sorted through it without actually looking at each envelope. "I met up with Simon Cortez this morning and installed some upgrades at his newest housing development. Took a lunch break and headed back to do the rest. Routine stuff."

"Where'd you go for lunch? You didn't eat alone, did you? You need to get out more." She twirled a dark curl around her finger over and over, a dead giveaway that she was fishing for a detail she could use to push him into dating.

He fought the surge of guilt lying to his kids would bring

and compromised with a half-truth. "I had a meeting with a client who needs an updated home security system. Nothing fancy. Deli sandwiches. I didn't want to ruin my appetite for dinner."

Her sigh and the way she glanced at her brother convinced him she'd accepted his glossed-over answer, which meant he needed to change the subject.

"I need to do a little paperwork and change clothes before we go eat. Let's plan on leaving at five fifteen." He headed toward his office before they could trick him into revealing more.

Hissed whispers carried to his ears as he backtracked to retrieve his computer bag, but Syd and Wil didn't summon him back to the kitchen for a more thorough inquisition. They might, however, try to corner him over dinner.

Cerise and I aren't dating, so there's nothing to tell.

When he settled at his desk and waited for his computer to boot up, his mind wandered to the XXX-rated activities he'd engaged in with the brainy sex goddess. Under normal circumstances, she would've been way out of his league, but their casual hookups didn't include parameters like net worth and bank account balances. They were about sex and mutual satisfaction mixed with a bit of unexpected chemistry. Jesus, he and Cerise had plenty of that.

Shaking off his thoughts, he typed in his password to update his scheduled and completed projects spreadsheets. A notification popped up from his payroll software that his four employees had recorded their hours, giving him another task to complete. After adding his labor to the latest Cortez Home-builders invoice, he emailed it to Simon and his company's accountant. The steady income from that particular source had funded Syd's college education and would do the same for Wil.

Done working for the day.

Dressed in jeans, a thermal shirt, hiking boots, and the coat that carried enough of Cerise's scent to make his dick half hard, he herded his kids to the truck a few minutes later. They dropped subtle hints about him inviting someone to go with him to the fortieth birthday party Rodney's wife was throwing for him in early April, the invitation for which they'd found in the mail he'd gotten yesterday.

As he pulled into a parking space at the restaurant, the more and more blatant attempts to coerce him finally stopped, allowing him to drop the threat of turning the damn truck around. "Let's go eat barbecue and ask the waitstaff to sing the birthday song to your brother, Syd."

She snorted a laugh and headed inside. Not waiting for usual welcome, she stepped up to the greeter stand. "Table for three please."

The guy about his daughter's age nodded once, grabbed some menus, and motioned for them to follow. "Right this way."

Syd and Wil trooped after him, with Dixon bringing up the rear. No sooner did he sit across from his kids than a raucous hoot of laughter snagged his attention.

Six women stood near the entrance—two with different shades of red hair, two with brown, one with black, and a blonde he could identify in the dark with his hands tied behind his back. Her gaze caught on his for a split second, sending his insides whirling and sparking a twinge in his dick. Then the group trailed after the young man who'd seated him and his kids. The taller redhead—Poppy, the woman Dixon was fairly certain Simon had slept with and wanted to date—waved his direction and said something to the seater. The guy nodded and gestured toward the table a few feet from Wil's chair.

Dixon's pulse jumped and his jeans tightened at the zipper when the women gathered near his son instead of settling at their six-seater.

Rose, the owner of Bell Lumber and one of his former clients, gave his daughter a brief hug. "Girlie, how are you? How's school? I haven't seen you in so long."

"Great, Mrs. Holloway. It's good to see." Syd's expression turned hopeful. "Is Meg home for break this week too? I'd love to get together."

Their chat continued while Dixon stood and offered a round of hellos to the rest of Cerise's friends. When he shifted his focus to her, embers ignited in every part of his body. "Cerise, did you have a chance to check that day and time I mentioned at our lunch meeting?"

Her eyebrow rose a hair, but no one seemed to notice. "Yes, it works."

"Good, I'm anxious to get started on the project." Honestly, he was more than anxious to explore new ways to bring her pleasure and more positions to find his own. He drowned in those intelligent brown eyes for another second before the server appeared and broke the spell.

CHAPTER NINE

GLAD HER BACK WAS TO DIXON'S TABLE, CERISE TRIED TO follow the story her friend Carnie was telling about a loser who got kicked out of The Ringer Saloon last night. It beat thinking about how many hours until her next sex fest with the slightly nerdy dad who knew how to play her body for maximum orgasms. She might've taught him plenty about the products she sold while they were snowed in, but he had a natural aptitude for bedroom skills.

Attentive. Creative. Thorough.

His low chuckle from not far behind her seat rippled down her spine, but the accompanying giggles and snorts from his kids told her they adored him for who he was, not what his money could buy them. Bradley and Tony had spoiled their children rotten, turning them into entitled adults without an ounce of humor or kindness. Dixon's ex didn't sound much better. Too bad she hadn't met the offspring of her late husbands before the weddings. Her response to their proposals probably would've been very different.

What if—

No, she wasn't going there. Regrets might be part of life,

but she refused to dwell on things she would certainly change if she could. Besides, do-overs would bring new disappointments and complications. Banging body parts with a smart and likable man was as good as life would get for her.

Poppy leaned closer on her left. “How can you stand it? The guy you’re screwing around with is *right there*.”

Movement beyond Scarlet on the opposite side of the table saved Cerise from having to respond to that unanswerable question and made Poppy’s observation all the more relevant.

Simon weaved past several other diners, pausing to speak to those he obviously knew, and sidled up to their group. His gaze seemed to linger on Cerise’s redhaired friend, but he smiled toward each woman at the table. Then he rested his hand on the top rail of Poppy’s chair. “Hi, ladies. I didn’t expect to run into you tonight, not that I mind. Lots of brains and beauty in one place. All small business owners. It’s good to see you supporting each other. I’ve never understood why some women would rather treat their peers like competition.”

Carnie, who was out of his direct line of sight, rolled her eyes. “What brings you to The Vinery, Mr. Cortez? Casing the joint for your next prospective date?”

A flush of color swept across Poppy’s cheeks and her jaw tightened.

Cerise gave her friend’s hand a squeeze under the table. “If he’s as smart as we are, he knows better than to flirt with any of us. We’re all willing to hide the body, no questions asked.”

Simon grinned and shook his head, although something in his expression said he wasn’t exactly carefree. “This isn’t flirting. It’s being friendly with the people I know. I’ll admit I enjoy talking to fairer sex. However, I’m not a cheater. I took myself off the market two years ago for the woman I’m going to marry. Someday. She just isn't ready for me yet, but I'm willing to wait for her. As long as it takes."

Poppy raised her water glass to her mouth, but it didn't disguise the color draining from her cheeks from Cerise's angle.

Is he serious?

A trio of pings in quick succession broke the silence that followed his announcement, and Poppy pivoted to grab her purse from under the coat on the back of her chair. After sliding her cell from the outside pocket and scanning the screen, she pushed to her feet, forcing Simon backward. "I have to go. My mom's on her way to the hospital."

He glanced toward the other side of the dining room and at Poppy again, a concerned frown replacing his wide smile. "I—"

"I'll drive you since you rode with me." Determined not to let anyone add to her friend's stress level, Cerise stood, shoved her arms into her jacket sleeves, and slung her purse on her shoulder. A hot flash rushed across her chest, between her shoulder blades, and up her neck, but she clutched Poppy's arm and urged her toward the exit. "Goodnight, everybody. I'll text when we know what's going on."

Not waiting for a chorus of acknowledgment, she hurried past the tables and out the doors, her friend in tow. Guilt should've smothered her as she rushed to her car. Instead, relief at not having to interact again with Dixon in public washed over her. Memories of their lunchtime tryst and how unexpectedly mind-blowing part-D-in-part-V sex with him had been still triggered aftershocks and the desire for more—much more—of the same in every possible position.

The worst aspect of the whole thing was she liked him, and that road led straight to hell.

❧

CERISE SET THE COFFEE CUP AND TAKEOUT BAG WITH breakfast on the side table and gathered Poppy close for a long hug. "Call or text if you need anything. More food, a change of clothes, someone to sit with you. Anything. Understand?"

"Thanks. I appreciate it more than you know." Her friend's teary response brought back memories of being alone in the hospital when her own mother had been at death's door.

I wouldn't wish that on my worst enemy, let alone one of my best friends.

After another quick squeeze, Cerise pointed at the delivery she'd made. "Try to eat something if you can. Carnie should be here any minute to sit with you, Rose will be here by noon with lunch, Sienna will be here at five with supper, and I'm just a speed dial away. Scarlet's wrangling your cleaning schedule."

Poppy's nod was less decisive than usual, but she had good reason to look defeated. "Go, before I start crying again."

You're allowed to cry, my friend.

Cerise kept the words to herself, since they weren't necessary or helpful, and stepped into the hallway of the hospice care center Mrs. Gardner had been transferred to early this morning. The muffled theme song from *Magic Mike* alerted her to a call as she cut across the lobby, and she fished her phone out of her coat pocket without slowing.

A swarm of rabbit vibrators hopped with wild abandon in her churning stomach when the name on the screen confirmed the caller, but she answered anyway, in case the call was about the installation of security system upgrades at her house. “Hello, Dixon.”

“Hi. I heard about Poppy’s mom. Is there anything I can do to help?”

His offer warmed her insides, even though the wind swept down her collar as she passed through the automatic doors to the parking lot. “It’s a waiting game right now, although the doctor’s saying she only has a few weeks at most. The rest of us are circling the wagons and have everything covered at the moment. We’re taking turns bringing Poppy whatever she needs, so she can spend as much time at the hospice center as possible.”

“Then what can I do for you? I’m guessing you stayed up all night with her so she wouldn’t be alone. My morning appointment just canceled and I’m free until twelve thirty. A massage and a few orgasms will help you nap better. Unless you’re working all day.”

She hit the unlock button on her key fob, ducked into the driver’s seat, and shut out the cold. Temptation proved too strong to resist his proposition. “I arranged for my assistant manager and one of my part-timers to cover for me today. Meet me at my house in twenty minutes.”

“I’ll be waiting there for you in ten.” His rumbly voice traveled over her skin, through her lower belly, and to her perked-up nipples. “And, Cerise? We’re going to need more room than that couch has. I suggest a bed. King size if you have it. See you soon.”

“Okay.” A deep breath did little to calm the anticipation thrumming in her veins. He wasn’t supposed to take care of her, except in the sexual way.

She ended the call and focused on getting to her house in one piece. The mix of exhaustion, horniness, and unexpected gratitude kept her alert on the drive home. Men had always bought her gifts and then had certain expectations in return, not that she'd really minded. Good sex wasn't something to complain about.

Unlike her husbands and former boyfriends, Dixon treated her like a person. She'd been a trophy, a prize, arm candy with a brain to Tony and Bradley and many others. Her new lover had none of those ambitions. He was more worthy of her time than any man she'd ever dated, and he hadn't pushed her to surrender more than she was willing to give.

Tossing aside her weird analytical reflections, she flipped on her signal and turned into her driveway. At the keypad, she punched in her code—0-0-6-9-0-0. The gate rolled to the left, paused for the count of ten, and rolled shut behind her.

A flash of red through the trees told her Dixon had arrived before his truck came fully into view, setting off a chain reaction of tingles, desire, and a bit of worry that she might be in over her head. He climbed out of his pickup as she tapped on the control for the garage door and then stepped up to her car door as she shut off the engine. The concern on his face was an exact match for his expression at finding out his son had been in an accident when they'd been snowed in.

Her stomach did a flip and her muscles wanted her to stay put, but she grabbed her purse and keys and tapped the unlock button. The door swung wide.

He reached for her hand and gently pulled her to her feet. "Did you have breakfast?"

She nodded, dodging what looked like an attempt to greet her with a kiss by pretending to juggle her keys. Intimacy of that nature had no place in their booty calls, especially when she was at her weakest. "Let's go inside."

With his palm at her lower back, he walked with her into the lower-level mudroom. "More than coffee? I can make something for you while you hop in the shower. Or a bath if you'd rather soak for a while."

His thoughtfulness slithered under the armor she always wore around men, but she couldn't summon the energy to bury him in her usual snark. "I had yogurt and a mini bagel with my coffee when I went to find food for Poppy this morning. My bedroom is upstairs."

"An invitation I can't refuse." At the bottom of the stairs, he helped her out of her coat, shed his own, and hung them both on the coat tree. "Lead the way."

CERISE'S BEDROOM RESEMBLED THE WINTER SKY. THE PALEST hint of gray covered the walls, and see-through strips of white fabric hung like tied-back curtains from a delicate scroll frame attached to the ceiling directly above the bed. An area rug with charcoal and white swirls extended beyond it on whitewashed plank flooring. Even the comforter was a shade of gray.

Where were the splashes of color that defined her?

He followed her into her personal space, unable to reconcile the extreme contrast between the woman he knew and the room. None of the house really suited her personality, vitality, or sexuality. The bland neutral walls and furniture presented the staged-property appearance of a model home.

Aiming toward what was likely the master bath, Cerise paused by a closed door to remove her red suede ankle boots. "It's boring, isn't it? This was husband number one's favorite get-away-from-the-city place for dinner parties. Guests stayed overnight sometimes, but we always headed back to the mansion. I never got around to redecorating after I moved in.

It always seemed…temporary. A shower sounds great, especially if you join me."

The slightly unsettled feeling in his gut dissipated with the sudden knowledge that she hadn't become a widow in this bed—or house.

He kicked off his shoes beside hers and dug for the strip of condoms he'd stowed in his pants pocket. "It would be my pleasure. And yours, of course."

She cast an inviting glance over her shoulder as she entered the bathroom with the same gray-and-white color scheme. "I'm counting on it. Get naked while I turn on the water."

Happy to let her take charge for now, he shed his clothes and helped her take off the breast-hugging sweater and form-fitting jeans she'd worn to The Vinery last night. A few subtle brushes of his fingertips in strategic places earned him soft sighs and goose bumps.

Grasping her hand, he guided her into the massive walk-in stall, mesmerized by her curves and honesty.

He set aside the foil packets, rubbed a palm full of body wash into a lather, and spread the bubbles over her perfect breasts. Her nipples pebbled with each gentle circuit, but he moved on to her arms and back and belly.

She closed her eyes and arched into his touch. "Mm. Feels good."

"Hold on to me while I wash your pretty feet." Using a firm touch, he ran his fingers along her arch and between her sexy toes, careful not to tickle or press too hard. Then he lowered her leg with a gentle glide over her calf and thigh before moving on to the other one.

Since she seemed comfortable with only the sounds of the steady sluice and splash of the spray, he stayed silent and moved on to her neat dark-blonde triangle, her slippery folds, and the crease between her ass cheeks. Her grip on his shoulders tightened as he slicked the fingers of his left hand over her clit and teased her opening. His right hand ventured farther back to the puckered hole he'd bumped over as he washed her.

She hummed and pushed against the fingertip, encouraging him to slide past the snug ring he'd explored in the dark last week. Her breath stuttered with each swipe over her swollen bud and glide into her tight ass.

He changed up the rhythm, adding a dip into her sweet pussy between flicks of her swollen nub and sucked a gorgeous nipple into past his lips. He tongued the bud and switched to give her other breast equal attention. Within seconds, her body jerked and an utterly feminine groan echoed off the walls. He slowed but didn't halt the synchronized motions, hoping to draw out her orgasm a little longer.

Her throaty moans tapered off and she rested her forehead against chest. Her panting breaths feathered over his pecs, driving his need to bury himself inside her to new heights. "Fuck me, Dixon."

After a quick wash of his hands, he suited up, shifted her to face him, and lifted her against the tiled wall. She wrapped her legs around his hips, letting him guide his dick into place. The fit of her still pulsing muscles around him threatened his control, but her pleasure was his focus. "Let it all go. The exhaustion. The stress. Just feel. Come again, Cerise, with me this time."

She tipped her head and parted her lips as he pumped into her welcoming body with slow, even strokes. Her changeable eyes became more green than brown beneath her heavy eyelids. "Don't stop."

He plastered his chest to her flushed breasts and nibbled a path up her neck to her ear. "Not stopping. Fuck, this gets better every time. Squeeze my cock. Jesus, just like that. Show me how much you want to come. Let me feel your pussy. God, I'm so close. Now."

Her muscles gripped him as she convulsed around him, wringing him dry while he growled into her shoulder. She trembled in his arms, clearly as overcome by her release as he was.

Tremors shook him to the core for several minutes, but he held her tighter, despite the strength that had drained from arms. Her head had dropped to his shoulder and her harsh breaths finally settled into rhythmic puffs that matched his own. Under different circumstances, he would've gone all in with her, ready to take their benefits to a whole new level.

We're both too damn jaded.

A twinge of disappointment tried to take root, but he snuffed it out. He wasn't in the market for a real relationship any more than she was.

He eased back and lowered her to floor. After tossing the used condom in the trash can, he shuffled them under the spray, wetting and washing and rinsing her silver-blonde silk. By the time he dried them both, gently combed her hair, and carried her to bed, she was boneless in his arms.

Not bothering to fold back the covers, he laid her on the sea of gray. She rolled to her stomach and the steady rise and fall of her back told him she'd fallen asleep.

Despite wanting to stretch out beside her, he kept his promise of a massage then dressed and headed home without kissing the mouth he hadn't yet tasted. She'd had enough trauma waking next to two dead husbands. He wouldn't risk scaring her away.

CHAPTER TEN

GIVING HER PHONE THE STINK-EYE, CERISE TAPPED HER fingernails on her desk and cursed her ridiculous brain for fixating on the lack of a response to her text message. She refused to obsess over a man's attention. Dixon had distracted her from hospice memories with multiple orgasms and an amazing massage that had relaxed her into the deepest sleep she'd had in a decade. So what if she'd awakened alone?

Alone is better than with a deceased lover.

What if he decided Wednesday's booty call replaced today's?

She snorted at the impossibility. He wouldn't pass up sex without strings. No man would.

The five-minute warning chimed on her laptop, alerting her to the video call with a potential website designer and manager for her online store. She logged in to the hosting site and clicked on the link to her scheduled meeting. Less than a minute passed before the student her favorite grad school professor had recommended requested entrance to the interview.

Early. That's a good sign.

The young woman appeared on the screen with an overflowing bookshelf and an open box of Cheez-Its in the background. Her name—Sydney M.—confirmed the name that had been in Dr. Birken's email. "Hi, I'm Sydney. Thanks for opportunity to talk with you today, Ms. Wethers."

Determined to be her usual professional self, in spite of her frustration, Cerise straightened her spine and adjusted the legal pad and pen in front of her. "Hi, Sydney. It's nice to meet you. Dr. Birken said you're looking for a summer internship with the possibility of future employment. Tell me about yourself. What made you decide to double major in Computer Science and Business Management? What about the Entrepreneurship certificate? What career interests do you have, beyond working with me to create and launch an e-commerce branch of my store?"

Tucking a loose strand of wavy dark-brown hair behind her ear, Sydney donned the excited smile of an early twenty-something-year-old set to graduate in the summer with two degrees. "Well, I'm twenty-one, almost twenty-two. I live in Bell, so meeting in person won't be an issue, if you prefer that. My dad started out as a software engineer and has run his own tech company for about ten years, so I grew with all the geek-speak language and learned how to build a computer when I was twelve. He also talks a lot about invoicing and payroll and everything related to the business side of things. We've discussed expanding his services, and my long-term goal is to take over the company when he eventually retires. But first, I need to gain some practical experience so I know what it's like to be an employee and a boss. When people like their jobs, they're happier and more productive."

Satisfied with her applicant's motives and drive, Cerise tackled the subject most likely to cause an issue. "What do you know about my enterprise?"

Sydney's expression didn't slip an inch, nor did her cheeks flush bright pink. "You opened BOB's Pleasure Palace, an adults-only store with sensual aids and products, two years ago in Bell as a small business with one location. Since that time, you've sold six franchises in Ohio through a very selective process. Your interest in an online store suggests a healthy bottom line and a bigger demand than you can keep up with in the physical stores."

"I'm impressed by your research." Cerise ignored the remaining questions on her list and moved on to one that popped into her thoughts during the young woman's recitation. "What do you believe the purpose of BOB's Pleasure Palace is, besides an income stream, which isn't even in my top five reasons?"

"To empower women and encourage the freedom to explore our sexuality without judgment or negative influence." Confidence glowed in Sydney's face and posture, like she had no doubts whatsoever about her statement. "And to challenge those who think women's bodies are strictly for men's pleasure and propagation of the human species. Making people uncomfortable is a not-so-unexpected bonus."

A truly genuine laugh burst out of Cerise. Sydney M. was a younger, slightly more subtle version of herself and would be the perfect addition to her team. "That's very true and you're absolutely correct. You've definitely done your homework. Have Dr. Birken send over the necessary paperwork to set up your internship. Your understanding of my business plan is nearly equal to my own, and I look forward to working with you, Sydney."

"You mean… Oh my gosh! I get to be your intern?" With wide eyes and a wider smile, Sydney fist-pumped the air. "This is freaking amazing. Thank you so much. I'll make sure the forms are emailed on Monday morning. Wow. Thank you, Ms. Wethers. I can't wait to work with you."

Unable to keep from grinning at her intern's enthusiasm, Cerise relaxed into the desk chair. "You're welcome. I'm looking forward to working with you and seeing what ideas you have. Once all the forms are taken care of, we'll chat again. In person, if you're available. If not, we'll do another video call. Do you have any questions for me?"

"I, um." Uncertainty clouded Sydney's previous eagerness. "I can't think of any right now, but I just want to say you've been the best role model since you opened your business. My mom travels a lot for her job, so we're not close, and you seem like… I guess I wish she was half as supportive as you seem to be. It means a lot to me."

Words jumbled in Cerise's brain for what felt like a full minute before she managed to piece together a reply. "I appreciate the compliment. She's missing out."

Sydney's face brightened. "Thanks."

Buzzing on the desk saved Cerise from the suddenly awkward conversation. "I need to take a call, but we'll talk soon. It was nice to meet you."

"You too, and thanks again. Bye." The square where Sydney had been vanished on the screen.

Cerise ended the meeting as she chanced a peek at the caller's name on her phone. Her insides scrambled as she swiped to answer. "Cerise Wethers."

"Shit, you're pissed off at me, aren't you? I was planning to confirm our meetup tonight when I left for my first appointment this morning, but one of Rodney's kids needed a trip to the emergency room, so I've been covering his jobs and mine all day. I'm on my way to the last one. How many orgasms will it take for you to forgive me?"

She shook her head and didn't even try to fight the smirk

his groveling inspired. "Hm. I may have to think about that for a few minutes."

"I'm pretty sure I can get six or seven out of you in two hours. Eight if we count simultaneous clit and G-spot orgasms. Those look so damn sexy on you. I can be at your house by six." His coaxing tone might've made her roll her eyes if she didn't know he was serious.

She pushed to her feet and walked to the storage closet, not willing to let him off the hook yet. "That's only four an hour."

"How about if we start now? I'll talk to you while you touch yourself right now."

"You need to keep both hands on the wheel, Dixon. That means no jacking off while you're driving." His low chuckle tickled her belly, and she sighed. "Besides, I don't need help with self-induced orgasms. I want your cock and your tongue and your hands."

He groaned. "And I have a hard-on when I'm almost at a service call. You play dirty. I wouldn't want you any other way. See you at six at your place?"

❧

AN EXPANSE OF SMOOTH SKIN TEMPTED DIXON TO GO FOR another round. Unfortunately, chimes from the grandfather clock in the formal living room rang out, carrying through the house to the bedroom. At the eighth peal, he grunted and rolled to the edge of the mattress. The walk to the bathroom required more effort than before their two-hour playdate, a reassuring sign he should leave.

At the bed, his boxer briefs and pants fought back when he pulled them on, as did his shirt. "I have to go. I promised my daughter we'd spend some time together tonight before she heads back to campus tomorrow."

Cerise peeked at him through the gorgeous mass of sex-tangled blonde hair and a satisfied sigh left her lips. "I think you wore me out, for tonight anyway. I didn't think that was possible."

He tried to pull on his sock and failed. Another attempt while sitting on the armchair in the corner succeeded. "No, you wore me out."

His dick twitched at her throaty chuckle, clearly not as worn out as the rest of him, but he finished dressing instead of succumbing to its spark of interest.

She shoved the pillow under her hips aside. "Let's call it a draw."

After a last caress of her shapely calf, he walked backward toward the doorway. "Monday at noon?"

A smirk appeared when she shifted to her back, giving him a spectacular view of her rosy nipples and the tasty treat between her thighs. "Monday. You're on the menu for lunch. Safe drive."

"Always. I'll lock up on my way out." He forced himself into the hall, not slowing until he stood at the driver's side of his truck. His attention tried to stray to the lighted windows on the second floor, but he rounded his truck and unlocked the door.

Keep moving. No distractions.

He'd promised Syd some family time this evening and he didn't break promises to his kids. Wanting to spend an entire night in Cerise's bed wasn't an option and it shouldn't even be on his radar.

He climbed in, started the engine, and drove out the private drive without a backward glance.

Yes, he enjoyed being with her, sexually and as someone

to talk to. She was smart, sassy, and sexy. What wasn't to like?

His gut insisted there was more to it than he wanted to admit. He liked her—as a friend, as a lover, as maybe something more. The problem was the something more. They had an agreement, and dating wasn't part of it. Romantic feelings also weren't part of it, no matter how much he looked forward to being with her, talking with her, connecting with her.

A Cortez Homebuilders pickup pulled into the intersection of the four-way stop a mile from home, reminding him of the conversation he'd had with Simon about women and marriage. While he wasn't a fan of the term "wife shopping," he certainly understood not being able to get a woman out of his system after a hookup and multiple repeat performances. Cerise was approaching the latter point—and that could become a major obstacle in their non-relationship.

He no sooner tapped the button to open the garage door than the familiar headlights of his daughter's car shone in his rearview mirror. He'd hoped for a few minutes to comb his hair and wash off Cerise's scent off him.

And the smell of sex.

Maybe she won't notice.

He snorted as he closed the door behind him.

Syd noticed everything—a beard trim, mismatched black socks, the couch moved an inch closer to the end table. She was a details person, and she wouldn't miss a thing.

Keys in hand, he let himself into the house and headed straight for his bathroom. After a few splashes of water on his face and a quick swipe of his fingers through his bedhead, he paused at his dresser long enough to dump his wallet and keys on top of it and kick off his shoes.

"Hey, Dad, where'd you go?"

He followed her voice to the kitchen instead of immediately answering.

Lie, bend the truth, or throw myself under the bus?

Her gaze landed on him when he accidentally bumped the stepladder as he rounded the corner at the pantry. "I was putting away—"

"Oh my god, you had a date, didn't you?" She set the jar of popcorn kernels next to the popper and jumped up and down while she clapped. "That's awesome! Who is she? Are you going out with her again? This is so exciting! I have news too."

"What kind of news?"

Any hope that his attempt at redirection fooled her dissipated with her eye-roll. "You spill first. Then I'll tell you about my day."

Changing directions, he walked to the refrigerator and grabbed the jug of milk. His stomach was going to need it. "I had to make a late house call for a client. No date."

All true.

"Then why do you have a lipstick smear on your collar? Huh?" Her mouth curved upward, like she'd caught him redhanded.

Grateful to have a valid explanation, he raised his left thumb. The Band-Aid covering his knuckle was loose from half a day's work and soaked from washing away the stickiness from going down on Cerise, but it hadn't fallen off. "It's blood. I sliced open my thumb on a job this afternoon."

She huffed out a noisy sigh. "Not the red spot. I'm talking about the coral lip-shaped one on the other side. Why are you so afraid to admit you went out with someone? If anything, it's about freaking time you had a life outside of being a businessman and a father. But…I guess if you don't want to tell me about, there's nothing I can do to convince you. You keep your secret, and I'll keep mine."

Frustration gathered in his chest. "Fine. I met someone. We're getting to know each other, but it isn't serious and might not ever be."

Going back to her task of making popcorn, she added oil and kernels to the popper and put on the lid. "And that's okay. I'm just glad you're socializing. There's nothing with having an active sex life over forty. In fact, it's great exercise."

Heat climbed up his neck to his cheeks. "I didn't say we were sleeping together."

She raised her eyebrows at him. "Dad. Seriously? You've been more relaxed this week than I've ever seen you. During winter break, you were stressed out about Mom saying she planned to visit for a couple days at Christmas. When you said she knew about Wil's stitches, you shrugged it off, like it was no big deal. You must really like this woman. Wil and I are happy for you."

"So you've had a discussion about this?" He tried to accept the fact that his kids knew he was getting laid and couldn't. They weren't supposed to know stuff like that about him.

"Yep." She plugged in the popper and leaned against the counter. "Since I know your big secret, I can tell you mine. I got an offer for a summer internship. Once the paperwork is done and approved, I'll fill you in on the details. Now go set up the videogame of your choice, so I can kick your butt."

CHAPTER ELEVEN

Three weeks with a steady diet of giving and receiving orgasms was heaven for Dixon's body, but his heart had decided it wanted to be involved in the fun. Every hot and heavy hookup left him wanting more of what he and Cerise had agree to leave out of the equation. The damn touchy-feely part of him would more than likely ruin the very good thing he had going on, especially since he'd tried to kiss her—on the lips—several times and she'd ducked her head or dodged his attempts some other way.

His cell buzzed next to the remains of his plate of eggs and toast, sending his gut cartwheeling and his pulse into overdrive. He flipped his phone over and the rush of anticipation deflated when his daughter's name appeared instead of Cerise's.

I'm in so much fucking trouble.

He swiped to answer the call and switched to speaker. "Hey, Syd. You're calling early. Everything okay?"

"Better than okay. My internship is official as of this morning. I just got an email from my professor. That means, unless I really screw up, I'll also have a job when I graduate at the end of the summer session."

Despite having the utmost confidence in his daughter, a huge weight lifted from his shoulders. "That's great! Congratulations. Do I get to know the specifics now that the paperwork is done?"

"Of course. So, you know how I was looking for a business that's known for being woman and LGBTQ friendly, socially and environmentally conscious, body positive, etcetera? Autonomous, Inc. is all that, and the CEO… She interviewed me herself. I was a little intimidated at first, but she's really down-to-earth and straightforward. She liked my answers to her questions and the research I'd done on her small business. She also founded a nonprofit that provides scholarships and support for people escaping abusive situations. And she's planning to offer employment opportunities at her stores and franchises through the nonprofit. I'll be helping her launch the first online store for her company. You know, like building her website from the ground up and managing the marketing side once it's up and running. I get to be part of the whole process, from start to finish. Oh, and her physical store is in Bell."

No, it can't be.

The payment he'd received for the BOB's Pleasure Palace job had come from a parent company named Autonomous, Inc. Did Cerise own other businesses?

Just ask what the store is called.

He pushed his plate away and rested his elbows on the table. "It sounds like you impressed her. What's the store? Does that mean you'll be moving back home?"

"First, I know you're going to get a little weirded out because of the products the store sells, but she's catering to regular people with normal urges. Otherwise, humans would go extinct. Do you promise not to freak out?"

Only one business in Bell that he knew of fit that description. How was he supposed to continue seeing Cerise when his daughter worked for her?

"Dad? Are you freaking out? I'm hoping to rent an apartment in town so I can walk to work. It'll save money on gas and insurance. Plus, you and your girlfriend might want to have sleepovers once Wil goes off to college."

"Syd, I'm not talking to you about…adult sleepovers. It's Cerise Wethers' store, isn't it?" He didn't need her to say yes since his gut already knew.

"Yes, it's BOB's Pleasure Palace. The place where people, especially women, are free to explore their sexuality without judgment. Having sex and enjoying it is normal—for women and other gender identities, not just men. She supports empowerment and knowing our bodies."

Had the woman he'd been swapping benefits with chosen Sydney as her intern because of his connection to her? Worse still, was his daughter sexually active?

Don't think about it. Do. Not. Think. About. It.

He buried his head in his hands and drew in a deep breath. A long exhale relieved none of the tension in his neck and shoulders. "I know."

"Did I mention it's a paid internship? I'm really looking forward to it."

Hearing the hall bathroom door open and what was probably Wil's bedroom door close, Dixon removed his hands from his hair and straightened. "I'm proud of you, Syd. I need to head out to my first appointment, but we'll celebrate the next time you're home. Love you."

"I love you too, Dad. Have a good day at work. Talk soon."

The call ended, giving him a good reason to dump the rest of his coffee and get on the road to his seven thirty appointment.

After making sure Wil was moving fast enough to be on time for school, Dixon shrugged on his coat, snagged his computer bag, and left through the garage. The thirty-minute drive didn't help resolve his concerns or the feelings still trying to bubble to the surface, but his swamped schedule meant texting Cerise wasn't an option. The words wouldn't form to send her a message anyway. Maybe by noon his brain, his dick, and his heart would finally get their shit together and save him from sounding like a horny lovesick teenager with no concept of how complicated life could be.

CERISE DRUMMED HER FINGERNAILS AGAINST THE OAK surface of her home office desk as she finished chewing the last chunk of mango from her lunch. She'd weighed her options and made a decision, but Dixon was thirty-five minutes late and hadn't called or texted to let her know he had to cancel or was on his way.

This is why I should've known better than to think I have any control over my love life.

A snort escaped. When had she ever?

Admitting to herself she was ready for her sexual relationship with him to become something more had created another shitshow. To say she'd been taken aback by her feelings was an understatement. Discovering her new intern was Sydney Mayhew threw a sledgehammer into the mix.

And now he's ghosting me.

He'd clearly found out about her business connection to his daughter—niece?—and chosen to cut personal ties. Did he plan to renege on their deal to add more exterior motion sensors to her outdoor system too?

"Fuck it. I'm done." She gathered her lunch dishes to carry to the kitchen. The light on the upgraded surveillance panel for the main gate flashed as she stood, announcing the arrival of someone with the newly updated code. Her pulse kicked up and her stomach swayed. "I don't give a damn if it *is* him. I'm still pissed off and he doesn't deserve the benefit of the doubt."

The judgment was a little harsh, even for her, but she should've listened to her brain instead of her sex drive when they'd gotten snowed in. Her heart would get over the silly budding emotion trying to take root, and it would teach her that she was meant to be single—sexually and romantically independent—once and for all.

Taking her time, she rinsed her dishes and loaded them in the dishwasher. The sound of the doorbell carried to her office not long after as she slipped her arms into her coat sleeves. Then she slung her purse on her shoulder and stalked down both sets of stairs to the lower level, where another round of chimes followed her to the door into the garage. At her car, her cell buzzed in her trousers pocket.

On the off-chance her employee needed her assistance, she gave herself permission to check her messages.

"Sorry I'm late. I've been thinking about our arrangement and... Not sure I can explain in a text. I'm at the front door. Are you home?"

"And you couldn't take five seconds to tell me a half hour ago?" She shook her head and settled in the driver's seat.

Another vibration pulsed through her hip.

"If not, do you mind if I stop by the store? I need to talk to you about this. It's important."

Instead of responding, she used the app to arm the security system Dixon and his crew had completely overhauled last week, dropped her phone into the center console, and pressed the button on the visor. She backed out of the garage as soon as the door rose high enough not to scrape the roof of her car. Out of sight on the other side of the house from him, she waited for the door to close again before gunning the engine a bit harder than was probably wise on the wet pavement. Luckily, the tires didn't skid or squeal.

She approached the gate without looking back to see if the red TMI truck trailed her. Distant headlights reflected in the side mirror when the eight-foot wrought-iron fence bumped closed behind her, a sure sign he'd witnessed her dramatic exit and decided to follow her.

I don't care. I. Don't. Care.

His ringtone filled the interior of her car and his name appeared on the navigation screen as she turned left to take the shortest route to BOB's. Her thumb tapped the disconnect button on the steering wheel before she even made the intentional decision to do it. Evidently, it had more sense than she did.

More ringing tempted her to throw her cell out the window, but she ended the call twice more before she let it go to voicemail. If he chose to leave a message, she could choose to delete it without reading or listening to it.

She arrived in the rear parking lot as the damn thing pinged with a notification. On her way to the service entrance, she powered down the device and stuffed it in her purse. Her office would provide an excellent hideout while she dealt with the weekly data upload for her accountant and ignored the ache in her chest and the knot in the pit of her stomach. She didn't need or want an explanation for his cold feet, second thoughts, or back pedaling.

Her part-timer looked up from the restocking cart across

the stockroom, forcing Cerise to wave a greeting while she relocked the delivery door. "I'll be in my office."

Thankfully, the single mother of two pre-teens returned to what she'd been doing, allowing Cerise to slip into her private space, hang up her coat, and power on her laptop.

Ten minutes and no completed tasks later, her assistant manager knocked and peeked into the office. "There's a man with a chinstrap beard and moustache out front who's asking to see you. Do you want to talk to him?"

"I'm busy ans—"

"Avoiding me." Dixon stood directly behind her employee, looking over the flustered women's head through the doorway. "Five minutes. That's all I ask. Just let me apologize in person. Without an audience. Please."

Five minutes seemed excessive for an apology, especially since he obviously intended to put an end to their benefits and, by association, their friendship and business association. Of course, she hadn't ever become friends with any of the men she'd shared benefits with until the weather had all but forced her to get to know her tech expert. He'd grown on her, revealing playful and sensual sides of him that most people probably never saw.

We were compatible in ways I wasn't with anyone before.

She leaned back in her chair and tried to unclench her jaw. Then she gestured toward the seat on the opposite side of the desk. "Close the door and sit down. Two minutes. The timer starts now."

WELL AWARE OF HOW QUICKLY A HUNDRED TWENTY SECONDS would pass, Dixon stepped back to let the green-haired employee return to the front of the store before shutting the office door and dropping into the chair across from Cerise. As much as he wanted to scrape his fingers through his hair, he didn't. Instead, he flattened his hands on his thighs. "I apologize for not showing up at noon like we agreed on. I've been rethinking this…thing we've been doing. Not because I don't want to have sex with you anymore. I do. It's…more than that. I need to know if you offered Sydney the internship because of our relationship."

Her silvery blonde eyebrows dipped toward her eyes and she frowned. "I didn't even know her full name until I read through the agreement yesterday. Then I wasn't sure if she was your daughter or niece or some other relative. She earned that spot on her own, and I have major reservations about my involvement with you while I'm supervising her. You standing me up today justifies those feelings. If that's—"

"She's my daughter, and I should've known you'd be professional about agreeing to let her intern here. You just always surprise me. In a really good way. I want more than sex with you. I know we both said we weren't interested in anything else, but I've changed my mind. Or you changed my mind. I don't know. Whatever. We're really good together and I think I'm falling in love with you." His voice cracked over the final words, but he stared at her like the realization brought peace and relief, like he'd never been more certain of anything. "I'm not saying we should get married if we don't want to. We deserve some happiness and I really hope you'll give us a chance."

CHAPTER TWELVE

"Cerise Wethers is unavailable. Please leave a message at the tone."

Dixon scrubbed his hand over his face at the canned greeting and dropped his chin to his chest. She'd wanted time to think about his profession of love and his appeal to modify their previous deal to include dating. While her request beat an outright refusal, he'd been suffering in silence for five days—which didn't bode well.

She wouldn't simply disappear from his life without an actual rejection, would she?

Maybe that had been her plan all along. Maybe it was why she had pulled away every time he'd tried to kiss her on the mouth like a real lover.

A beep sounded in his ear, giving him no choice but to recite the words he'd planned to say to her. "Hi, Cerise. It's Dixon from TMI. I wanted to let you know Rodney will be out to install the additional outdoor motion sensors at three. He has the gate code, so you don't have to be home if you're not able to leave the store. You should change the code to something easy to remember but not too obvious after he's done to be on the safe side. I'll have him text you the instructions when he's finished. Let me know if you have any questions or concerns."

He ended the call and set his phone face down on his desk. It buzzed and hummed almost immediately, shooting his pulse sky-high and making a cold sweat race across his upper back and neck. Taking a slow breath to calm the rebellious bit of breakfast he'd eaten, he flipped over his cell with a shaky hand.

The spark of hope he couldn't suppress burned out in an instant at the name on the screen. He swiped to answer the call and lifted his cell to his ear. "Simon, what can I do for you?"

"Dixon. I have a few more upgrades for you when you get a free hour or two, and I could use some advice. Are you up for Mexican food and a beer later?"

He leaned back in the chair and closed his eyes. "I'll squeeze in the upgrades later this week, but I can't help you with the advice if it's about women, buddy."

"That doesn't sound good. Did you fall in love or something?" Simon's laugh suggested the question was a joke.

"Not funny. I don't want to talk about it. Six thirty at Benito's?"

"Damn. That bad, huh? Six thirty works. Be prepared to spill your story and try to help me with mine."

The call disconnected before Dixon could tell his friend not to hold his breath. Considering how little progress Simon had clearly made with his own problem, they should probably drown their sorrows in guacamole and queso.

Aware that he wasn't fit to deal with clients, he handed off three small jobs to one of his newer technicians and spent the morning and most of the afternoon sending quotes, answering emails, and preparing invoices.

As he shut down his computer, his cell sent his gut churning again. Disappointment and guilt battled when a message from Wil popped up.

"Hey, not sure if you remember from this morning, but I'm heading to Garrett's after track practice for pizza and studying. Home by 10. I'll text you when I'm leaving. Love ya, Dad."

He blinked away the bleariness in his eyes and tapped in his reply. *"It's been a long day, so I appreciate the reminder. Have fun. Be careful. Love you too."*

A wave of melancholy flattened him where he sat at the realization that his kids had their own lives to live and wouldn't be around every day for much longer. It was too much to take after the catastrophic banishment by Cerise.

Instead of stewing in his bad mood, he pounded out three miles on the treadmill, showered, and dressed in jeans and a TMI long-sleeved t-shirt. With death metal playing on the stereo, the drive to Benito's wasn't as bad as it would've been if depressing rock ballads had been the soundtrack. He pulled in the parking lot behind Simon's silver Cortez Homebuilders truck and parked beside it.

A nod sufficed as a hello for both of them on the walk to the entrance. They trailed after the greeter to a small booth, ordered drinks and food, and simultaneously sighed when their waiter hurried toward the other side of the restaurant.

Simon rapped his fingertips on the table until their chips, dip options, and beers arrived, a sign of how wound up he was about his not-quite-there girlfriend. "I'm guessing it's now common knowledge who I was talking about a few weeks ago, after I all but announced my intentions at The Vinery to Poppy and her friends. She looked like she was about to faint when I said I was waiting for her to be ready. And then she got the phone call about her mom. I haven't seen her since then, but I know she's gotta be having a really rough time right now. I want to be there for her and have no clue what to do or how to help without pressuring her."

His friend's word vomit took Dixon by surprise. The guy was typically more circumspect and succinct.

He sipped his slightly foamy draft while a list of ideas formed from his fairly limited experience. "I'm sure Cerise, Scarlet, Rose, Sienna, and Carnie have meals and the usual stuff like rides and visits covered. My mom scheduled a massage for a co-worker who was going through something similar. I think the woman's husband had cancer. What about books or music to keep Poppy occupied while she's sitting there with her mom for hours? Maybe fill her gas tank? Mow her yard?"

"Those are really good suggestions. Thanks." Simon seemed slightly more relaxed, but his easy smile was still missing. "What about you? I thought you swore off dating and marriage."

"I thought I had too." After another drink, Dixon set his glass on the cardboard coaster and slowly spun it in a circle. "You know how Cerise and I got snowed in at her shop? Things happened and then more things happened afterward by mutual agreement. She's snarky as hell, but that didn't stop me from wanting more than booty calls. In fact, the way she never pulls her punches is a huge draw. Her honesty. And she's so damn smart behind that sexy body. I told her I was falling in love with her and she hasn't spoken to me in five days."

"Jeez, we're pretty pathetic, aren't we?" Grabbing a chip from the basket, Simon frowned. "What are you going to do if she never calls?"

"I haven't decided." Dixon waited until the server delivered their food and left before he continued. "I'm not giving up without a fight. I know that much. There's a sensitive woman behind that blunt personality, whether she likes it or not."

❧

"GO HOME. YOU NEED TO EAT AND SLEEP. SITTING HERE WITH me for hours won't change anything, and it's just bringing back horrible memories of your mom being in hospice care." Poppy engulfed Cerise in a tight hug and then nudged her toward the hall. "I'll be fine by myself for a while before I head home for a good night's sleep. I promise."

"Are you sure?" Given the choice of remembering how helpless and alone she'd felt seven years ago or examining her feelings for Dixon, she preferred thinking about her mother.

"Cerise, seriously. I can deal with this." Her friend's stern look warned of a boot to the backside if she didn't leave. "And you need to face up to the fact that you care about—"

"Please don't say his name. I'm having a hard enough time as it is." Surrendering to Poppy's request, she passed through the open doorway. "Call me if you need anything."

A nod sent her down the quiet corridor, but the noise in her head got louder.

He can't be in love with me.

Yes, he can.

I can't be in love with him, either.

Since when are you a liar?

If she didn't love him, why did his silence—the silence she'd asked for—hurt so damn much?

She trudged through the dusting of new snow that covered the parking lot and climbed into her car. "Ugh. Why am I acting like a ridiculous teenager with a crush?"

Several vibrations hummed through the cup holder where she'd set her cell, jolting her heart. A group text from her friends triggered a groan. She was an idiot for feeling disappointed when Dixon had promised to give her all the space she wanted.

Poppy's unsolicited advice led the conversation, followed by Rose's, Carnie's, Sienna's, and Scarlet's. They all had sent basically the same message.

"Talk to him."

"Call him."

"Go see him."

"Tell him how you feel."

"Admit to him AND YOURSELF how you feel so you can get back to getting laid on the regular."

Evidently, her friends had no qualms about sticking their noses in her business, not that she hadn't shared quite a few details and done the same to them on numerous occasions.

A string of laughing-crying emojis popped up after Scarlet's two cents, and Cerise had to admit her rocket-scientist-turned-mechanic friend made a very good point.

But sex isn't all I want.

She leaned against the headrest and closed her eyes, hoping to stem the emotion threatening to overwhelm her. A frustrated scream got stuck in her throat and tears welled behind her eyelids.

Damn it, I'm not a crier. I'm not.

The wetness on her cheeks said otherwise, and she dug for a tissue in the center console. Dabbing at the damp trails did nothing to slow the dam trying to burst open. Instead of fighting it, she gave it free rein, mourning the loss of her mom in a way she hadn't since the night her only parent—her only family—had lost the battle with cancer. Would she still have dated and married Tony or Bradley under different circumstances?

Then they'd up and died on her while she'd been asleep next to them, the same as her mom. She hadn't let anyone that close again until Dixon.

Not true.

Her pair of late husbands had been a misguided attempt to prop herself back up, to not be alone. Despite their business standing and money, she hadn't let them lord their power over her in public or private. Neither had inspired more than superficial affection and a promise to uphold her wedding vows. They'd rewarded her for her loyalty, but she'd never loved them like Scarlet and Rose adored Nelson and Barton.

Dixon, on the other hand, she truly enjoyed spending time with. He treated her with respect and never expected her to perform to make himself look good. Their interactions were easy, not choreographed or awkward.

And I pushed him away.

Am I protecting my heart if I break it before he can?

Another worry nagged at her, one that was every bit as important. Had she broken his heart in the process of thinking she was protecting her own?

Her phone buzzed again as she mopped her face, the concealer she'd applied to disguise the dark circles under her eyes staining the tissue. Her waterproof mascara, however, didn't budge.

A message lit up the screen and then vanished when it darkened a second later. *"Are you okay?"*

A glance toward the building revealed the silhouette of someone standing at a window about halfway down the wing through the falling snowflakes. Poppy had obviously been watching to be sure she actually headed home.

They were sisters of a sort, always ready to support each other, as were the rest of their peri- and menopausal friends.

Family.

Cerise started her car and then typed in her own message. *"I will be after I have a talk with Dixon."*

❧

WIL'S NAME FLASHED ON THE NAVIGATION SCREEN AND HIS ringtone filled the cab at the same time Dixon turned into his driveway. He pressed the button to answer the call while the garage door slowly rose. "Hey, Wil. Are you coming home now?"

"Hi, Dad. Actually, I was calling to see if it's okay if I stay at Garrett's tonight. We still have another chapter to study and the snow's supposed to really start accumulating in the next hour. I'm not sure I'm comfortable driving in it at night."

"Good thinking, as long as it's okay with his mom and dad. I just got home from dinner with Simon Cortez and the roads are already getting a little slick, so there's a chance you'll have a school delay tomorrow." Dixon shut off his truck and closed the garage door. Then he snagged his keys and the takeout container with his leftover enchilada and lifted his cell to his ear as he headed inside.

"No worries. Garrett's mom suggested it."

"Be sure to tell her I said thanks for letting you stay and feeding you. Do you have a change of clothes in your gym bag? Or do you want me to run some over to you now?"

"I have everything I need."

"Okay." Flipping on the light switch, he walked into the mudroom off the kitchen. As he unzipped his coat, bells chimed from the front of the house. "Gotta go. Somebody's at the door. See you tomorrow."

"G'night, Dad. Thanks."

After a quick detour to stow his leftovers in the fridge, he stalked to the living room. Who would be ringing his doorbell at nine thirty on a snowy night? Had someone been in a weather-related accident on his street?

Rather than check his app to see who stood on his porch, he pushed aside the sheer curtain covering the narrow strip of glass to the right of the door.

Ice-blonde hair sparkled around a pinched face that looked ghostly pale under the security light. His heart leapt and his gut roiled at the sight of Cerise on the other side of the wall from him. Was she here to officially dump him or give him a reason to hope?

Sucking in a calming breath, he unlocked the door and swung it inward. Her red-rimmed eyes locked on his, sending his stomach to the ground. He cleared his throat. "What happened? Did Poppy's mom pass away?"

She shook her head and bit her lower lip. "Not yet."

"Come in and tell me what's going on." He reached for her, letting relief wash over him when she didn't pull away. Her gloved hand tightened around his, but he guided her into the entryway and helped her out of her coat instead of hauling her into his arms. "Let's go in the kitchen and get you something warm to drink. It's nasty out there tonight."

Her lack of a sassy comeback seemed like a good indication something pretty damn serious had happened.

Rather than pushing for answers, he pulled out a chair at the table for her and then set to work making two mugs of tea. "Is mint okay?"

"It's fine, but…"

"But?" With water heating in the electric kettle, he backtracked to the table and sat with their knees almost touching. "If you're not in the same place I am, just say so. That's my problem, not yours."

"It's my problem too." She met his gaze, glanced past him, and then looked him in the eye again.

He blinked at her, not entirely sure what she meant by that. "I'm not going to become a stalker or anything, if that's what you're implying."

Her frown and eye-roll confused him even more. "I know that. When would you have time to peek in my windows or follow me around town like a creeper? What I was trying to say was…I might… No, I *do* have feelings for you. Overwhelming, slightly annoying, scary-as-hell feelings that I didn't want."

"I didn't want them, either, but shit happens sometimes." He scooped her up and moved her to his lap so he could bury his face in her neck and finally take a full breath. When she looped her arms around him, holding on like she didn't plan to ever let go, all the tension and hopelessness of the past five days vanished. "I never thought I could fall in love again. And this feels a thousand times stronger than when I was twenty-two. God, scary as hell is accurate."

She lifted her head from his shoulder and rubbed her palms over his scruffy jaw. "There's something I've been wanting to do, but I'm not sure now is a good time."

He raised an eyebrow, his interest piqued. "Oh? What's that?"

"Kiss you. On the mouth. It felt too intimate before, but I'm ready now." She cast a fleeting look toward the living room. "Although, maybe we shouldn't start something we can't finish with your son here."

Not giving her or himself a second to overthink, he pressed his lips to hers for a far-too-short and far-too-casual peck. “There. The pressure’s off, and Wil’s staying overnight at a friend’s house. He called right before you got here. That doesn’t mean we have to—”

“Yes, we do. I missed you, and don’t you dare try to convince me to take things at a snail’s pace now that I’ve made up my mind.” The warning fell flat from the uncharacteristic tentativeness in her expression. Her admission, however, brought immeasurable joy.

“I missed you too.” The urge to carry her to his bedroom and make up for the days they’d spent apart was strong, but he vowed to let her lead. “You’re in charge. I’m not about to risk scaring you off again.”

“It’ll take more than this.” She lowered her mouth to his, starting with a light brush of her soft lips and then slipping her tongue inside when a grateful sigh escaped him.

Her invasion wasn’t rushed, and he savored learning this unexplored part of her. One smooth glide led into another and another, sweeping him farther away from the past. When she came up for air, he kissed her nose, her cheeks, and her forehead. “Still okay?”

“No. Take me to bed.” She tried to wiggle off his lap, but he kept her from escaping, although she didn’t seem to make much of an effort to get away.

As he pushed to his feet with her cradled in his arms, he captured her mouth again. With more than half his attention on kissing her, he stumbled out of the kitchen and down the hall to his bedroom, finally laying her out and following her down onto the mattress. Within seconds, their clothes landed in a haphazard pile on the floor, he’d rolled on a condom, and he was inside her—where he belonged.

Despite the desire raging through his body, he made slow, sweet love to her until they both gave in to the bliss that proved their chemistry, made their feelings clear, and righted their path. He dragged the comforter over top of them and breathed in the intoxicating scents of her hair and sex, treasuring the ability to hold her against him in the dim light of his bedside lamp. Her breathing evened out, but he hovered on the edge of wakefulness long after she fell asleep, listening to every calm sigh and subtle movement as she snuggled closer to him.

At least an hour passed before she raised her head and blinked at him. A hint of panic shadowed her face for a moment, passing quickly when she smiled at him. "You're here."

Hating what must be going on in her head, he rolled on top of her, careful to brace most of his weight on his elbows. "Yeah. I love you, and I'm not going anywhere. Not for a long, long time."

"I love you too." She caressed his back, her eyes now devoid of the fear. "I can't guarantee I won't feel terrified on occasion, but I trust you not to leave me. I might need to look into therapy about that, though. So, I, uh, was also sleeping beside my mom when she died from cancer, and I didn't even connect it to the other two times until Poppy pointed it out to me earlier tonight."

"God, Cerise, I can't even imagine how scary it was for you to wake up next to me." He hugged her as close as he could without crushing her. "I'm here if you want or need my support. We'll handle our issues together. Okay?"

She nodded. "Okay. How about if you start by loving me some more?"

Satisfaction, contentedness, and craving settled over him like a warm blanket. "That's the easiest thing in the world."

GET READY FOR THE NEXT STORY IN THE ROMANCING THE Phone series! *Telephone Lines*, featuring Poppy Gardner and Simon Cortez, is coming in Fall 2026!

THANKS FOR READING! IF YOU ENJOYED THIS STORY, PLEASE consider leaving a review on the retailer's website, BookBub, and/or Goodreads to help other readers find their next book! Join my Facebook reader group for fun discussions and subscribe to my newsletter to receive the latest news about releases, sales, book signings, and more.

TELEPHONE LINES SNEAK PEEK

Prologue

Two years ago

Despite being a bit tipsy from the steady flow of cheap champagne, Poppy Gardner was still of the opinion the monstrosity she wore looked like someone had puked up a hundred Pinkie Pie ponies all over her—with fluffy magenta chunks atop the Pepto-colored mess. Because that wasn't bad enough, it also clashed with her red hair and almost glow-in-the-dark pale skin. The hideous thing belonged in a toddler's dress-up trunk, not in a forty-nine-year-old woman's wardrobe.

She cast a last scowl at the restroom mirror to be sure none of the frothy layers of the skirt had gotten tucked into her underwear during her potty break. That would be the last straw. Why, oh why, had she agreed to be a bridesmaid in her cousin's wedding?

That's right. For an excuse to skip out on another high school reunion event. The lesser of two evils?

God, I'm burning this dress as soon as I get home tomorrow.

Satisfied she wasn't about to flash anyone, she marched back to the reception hall for a second piece of cake and a final best-wishes to the cousin she might never speak to again.

A meaty hand intercepted hers as she reached for the only redeeming quality of this over-the-top celebration. "Want to dance? You're Poppy, aren't you? The cousin who cleans toilets for a living?"

"Housecleaning business, actually." She extracted her wrist from the stifling grip with a quick twist and rolled her eyes at the turd who'd tried to grope her ass when he went through the receiving line. "I remember meeting you. DJ, who isn't a disc jockey. You suck shit out of septic tanks for your dad, right?"

His unibrow dipped over his alcohol-reddened nose, like he wasn't sure if she'd insulted him or not. Under normal circumstances, she would've had as much respect for his occupation as any other career.

Today? Not so much.

Behind him, her newest—and wealthiest—client snorted. What was the owner of Cortez Homebuilders doing at this low-brow event?

She picked up two servings of raspberry-filled white cake topped with miniature fuchsia roses made from whipped cream icing. "Simon, I was just about to come find you. Join me for dessert so we can discuss next week's schedule?"

Aiming an orthodontist's dream of a smile at her, he stepped in front of her accoster and nodded. His dark brown eyes held a hint of amusement, but his focus seemed to be entirely on the cleavage about to spill out of her dress. "Good to see you, Poppy. You know I'll never turn down an opportunity to chat with a fellow successful business owner."

The pat on the back was a good reminder that she'd grown her Clean As A Whistle customer list enough in the past year to hire two more full-time employees and upgrade both her computer and her recordkeeping system. With a little more luck and perseverance, she would be able to add even more staff in another six to eight months.

He snagged a pair of plastic champagne flutes from a passing server and gestured for her to lead the way to her table. Then he waited for her to wiggle past the cotton-candy fluffs on her ass to plop flat on the chair before he lowered himself into the seat closest to her. "Your dress looks… awkward for sitting."

"You can be honest." She cut through the thick layer of frosting and scooped up a mouthwatering bite. "It's just plain awkward. Pink is so not my color and fluffy is so not my style. I'm planning to—"

"Hey, folks!" Feedback screeched through the speakers, but the country band's lead singer drawled right through it. "Come join the newlyweds for the last dance of the evening before we send them off to the honeymoon suite!"

"—use it for kindling when I get home." She stuffed the forkful of sugary confection between her lips, letting it melt onto her tastebuds, and then washed it down with a healthy sip of the very dry bubbly Simon had set near her plate.. "Damn, this cake is amazing. The champagne, not so much. But wedding guests can't be choosers."

His broad grin and low chuckle triggered a shiver up and then back down her spine.

Okay. He's cute, but I'm not interested in being another float in the long parade of his conquests.

He lifted a respectable sliver of dessert toward his mouth.

"I'm usually a demi-sec person. Brut is a bit like drinking turpentine to me. But, as you said, we can't be choosers—unless we're drinking one of the really bad beer choices."

"That's sacrilege! I'm not ruining this cake with beer." She scrunched up her face and shuddered. "What the hell is demi-sec? One of those push-up bras that keeps the girls from drooping for the three minutes it takes to go slip-sliding down my ribs?"

He laughed again, the rich sound washing over her but also reminding her the man had a reputation for flirting with every eligible woman he met and having more first dates than the entire population of northeast Ohio. "Demi, meaning half. And sec, meaning sweet. Not dry, but not overly sweet. I have to agree that the beer offerings here would definitely ruin this cake. By the way, the groom's father has done some subcontracting for me and I know the groom from some business courses we had together in college. That's why I was invited. You were curious, weren't you?"

She shoveled in another bite of cake and shrugged, but heat crept across her chest, up her neck, and over her cheeks.

Grr. The curse of the redhead.

Thankfully, he didn't comment on it and finished his skimpy serving of dessert as the microphone squealed again. Hers, on the other hand, was long gone.

"Okay, folks, it's time to line up and wish the happy couple one more congratulations!"

Simon pushed away from the table, stood, and extended his hand. "What do you say we take advantage of a head start to the elevators before the mad rush?"

With a grateful nod, she let him help her to her feet. "Absolutely."

Tingles raced up her arm with the contact, but she stepped out of reach instead of yanking her fingers away from the electrical current. His palm at her lower back only made matters worse on the hike away from the ballroom. She quickened her pace to put some space between them, despite her toes aching from the awful shoes the bride had chosen.

Damn, she should've brought her own strappy sandals with her on this weekend trip.

Her heel caught on the carpet and sent her careening forward as she closed in on the turn to the bank of elevators. "Shit!"

Arms closed around her, catching her what seemed like mere inches before she would've face-planted on the lobby floor. Warm breath feathered across her exposed upper back, and another burst of electricity zipped through body. "You make those heels look amazing, but maybe you should carry them instead of wearing them."

Straightening, she kept hold of his shoulder for balance and then slipped off her shoes. "Stupid things were making my feet hurt anyway."

He somehow managed to hook the fingers of his right hand through the straps without letting go of her, which was probably a good thing since her equilibrium was a little off-kilter. "Do—"

"Where're you going, Poppy? Do you want to go get a drink in the bar?"

Simon tensed with the persistent septic guy's overly loud invitation and guided her toward their destination. "I'd like to make sure you get to your room safely. Is that okay?"

Touched by his protectiveness, she nodded. "Yes. Thanks. Otherwise, I might end up sleeping in a jail cell. I'm on seven."

The doors of the closest elevator whooshed open as he stabbed at the call button. His arm relaxed slightly when they stepped aboard, but he didn't let go, even after the doors slid closed again and he swiped his keycard to access the non-public areas of the hotel. "Great timing."

She patted his chest over the expensive-looking suit and tie he wore. "My hero."

His milk-chocolatey eyes darkened, drawing her into their fathomless depths, but his husky voice incited goose bumps in places she'd never experienced them before. "I'm pretty sure you wouldn't see me as a hero if you knew how badly I want to kiss you right now."

A little hanky-panky won't hurt, will it?

"I'd rather have that than a hero with no sense of adventure." Moving closer until they were toe to toe, she brushed her lips over his.

He hauled her against him and swallowed her gasp with a breath-stealing joining. His tongue invaded her mouth, exploring every inch like his life depended on it and igniting flames throughout her body. Calloused fingertips skimmed along her bare arms and shoulders and dove into her hair. Then his lips followed her jaw to her hairline and he licked the outer shell of her ear. When he sucked her earlobe between his teeth, heat streaked to her nipples and south to her clit.

A needy moan escaped as she nearly orgasmed on the spot. Gripping his head, she held him in place, hoping a repeat of the motion carried her up and over that barely out-of-reach ledge. "More."

A faint chime tried to distract her and then a husky canned female voice finished the job. "Seventh. Floor."

The doors whooshed open, but not before he put a good two feet between them. "Hold that thought. Room number?"

She blinked at him as she willed her brain to remember the simple information he'd asked for. "I, um…714, I think. Yes, 714."

Seemingly in complete control of his libido, he closed his hand around hers and led her out of the elevator and down the hall to her suite. At the door, he stood aside while she dug her phone from the wide sash at her waist and then found her room key in the hotel's app. When the green light flashed above the handle, he pushed it down and held the door open for her. He didn't, however, follow her across the threshold.

Disbelief and disappointment warred with each other as she waited for a sign he planned to pick up where they'd left off. Was he going to leave her to take care of the ache between her thighs herself? Or was he part vampire and needed an invitation to enter?

She frowned at him. "What do you think you're doing, working me up and quitting before the job's done? Get in here."

One corner of his talented mouth hiked upward, but he didn't hesitate to join her in the hall leading to the living area. "I'm not a quitter."

Taking charge of the situation, she wrapped her fist around his tie and walked him toward the couch. Had she ever in her life been so consumed with the need to get naked with a man before?

I think not.

Her shoes landed on the floor a step later and his mouth devoured hers again, his tongue tangling with hers while his fingers tugged at the zipper near the middle of her back. The near-silent *scritch* to the top of her ass and subsequent avalanche down her legs freed her from the bane of her existence. Then he lifted her out of the pink drifts and sat on the couch with her thighs straddling his hips.

When he broke away, rough panting tickled the skin above her breasts. "I want you so much, Poppy. I'm asking for your consent. If you don't want to—"

"Yes." She attacked his belt and the suit pants keeping them from fucking each other senseless. "I'll get the zipper. You have a condom, right?"

He twisted his arm behind him as he raised himself several inches off the cushion. His hand reappeared with his wallet. "Always."

In under thirty seconds, he was suited up, held her thong aside, and guided her onto his rigid length. His hardness stretched her neglected muscles with each unhurried inch, wringing a throaty moan from her. He grunted against her throat when he bottomed out. "Fuck. Ride me. Let me see you come apart."

She shivered at the words and vibrations and sensations zinging through her body. The first rock of her hips made him glide deeper and set off ripples of pleasure flowing through her lower belly. "God, that feels…"

He freed her left breast by yanking the cup of her strapless bra down with his teeth and then flicked his tongue over her nipple. "How does it feel, Poppy?"

"Ahh!" Tremors accompanied the lightheadedness the attention sparked, making thoughts and words impossible.

"And what about this?" He slicked his thumb through her folds and circled her clit.

She choked out another gruff sound, barely able to keep the back-and-forth motion on his rock-hard erection, but his free hand gripped her ass and helped her maintain the rhythm.

"Tell me, Poppy." His lips closed over her tight bud and his fingers stroked her bundle of nerves.

"Divine." Between his desperate-sounding request and his well-placed attention, an orgasm ripped through her in the next second.

At her breathless whisper, he flipped her to her back and sank into her, each thrust carrying her away and sending her to another plane of euphoria. Her mind shattered as she went into a higher freefall, surrounded by a rough voice shouting her name and the unexpectedly soothing heat of his body wrapped around hers.

Humid breaths created a sauna at her neck, but she didn't move, didn't try to escape from the comfortable weight holding her down. Sex had been mostly good with the handful of men she'd slept with in her life. This experience, though, revealed all she'd been missing. Even the toys in her nightstand drawer wouldn't live up to doing the deed with Simon Cortez.

STILL STUNNED BY THE CONNECTION HE'D DISCOVERED WITH Poppy last night, Simon splashed cool water on his face in her bathroom sink and sorted through his options. They were limited.

She would undoubtedly think he was losing his damn mind if he admitted to the struck-by-lightning feeling that had hit him out of nowhere. They'd known each other for two and a half months, since she'd bid on and won his first new-construction cleaning contract, so why had he failed to notice their chemistry?

No way in hell would he let her think she'd been nothing but a one-night stand, either.

Isn't there some middle ground?

Averting his gaze from the shower, where their second round of lovemaking had taken place, he returned to the bedroom. The king-size bed had hosted rounds three and four. The gift bag on the nightstand, courtesy of her cousin's bachelorette party, no longer contained any novelty condoms, only a deck of cards sporting mostly naked men and several packages of gummy cocks.

"So, um, last night…" With navy leggings and a snug t-shirt hugging her luscious curves and her gorgeous red hair gathered in a low ponytail, Poppy leaned against the dresser across the room and fidgeted with one of the handles. "I don't want it to affect our business relationship. We have a contract I can't afford to lose, especially if it means having to let go the new women I just hired. They don't deserve to pay for my unprofessional choices."

His stomach sank to his knees, but he nodded. "I understand. It makes perfect sense."

"We can go back to just being business acquaintances and…friends?" Her lower lip vanished behind her front teeth for several beats of his aching heart. "We're friends, aren't we?"

Coming Fall 2026!

ABOUT THE AUTHOR

Mellanie Szereto is the *USA Today* Bestselling Author of over sixty romcoms and contemporary romances, most with characters who have plenty of life experience like herself. Whether you call them older, seasoned, mature, experienced, or later-in-life protagonists, they deserve love too! Her stories are often set in small towns with quirky main characters, fun secondary casts, and lots of humor. She enjoys gardening, cooking, and baking—as well as hiking to work off the fruits of her labor—and incorporates food into all of her stories. She lives in an old farmhouse in rural Indiana with her husband of thirty-eight years.

Visit her website for more information about her books!

www.ingramcontent.com/pod-product-compliance
Lightning Source LLC
LaVergne TN
LVHW020047110826
845155LV00029B/666

* 9 7 8 1 9 4 2 5 2 2 9 5 9 *